Sara

Six

Strings

2

Sara Six Strings

Moriah Howell

This book is a work of fiction. Any references to historical
events, real people, or real locales are used fictitiously.
Other names, characters, places, and incidents are the
product of the author's imagination, and any resemblance to
actual events or locales or persons, living or dead, is entirely
coincidental.

Copyright © 2010 by Moriah Howell

To Sharon D., for reading, reviewing, and whisper screaming over Gavis' various outfits. Every time I see a fedora, I will think of you.

And to Sara B., who inspired the short story Sara Six Strings that turned into this slightly-longer novel. Thank you so much for everything.

Part One

Our story begins to unfold in a classic suburbia. Identical white houses line the impeccably clean street. The sounds of lawn mowers mingle with children's laughter. The late summer scene is painted in vivid colors, teeming almost overbearingly with Life.

Fathers are washing their expensive cars, cutting the grass with complex precision or throwing balls around with their young sons. Mothers sit on their porches in wide-brimmed hats, drinking iced tea or lemonade and gossiping with their friends. Children are holding hands and dashing together through temperature-moderated sprinkler systems.

Overall, this picture is one of absolute perfection. At least it is until you get to the end of the street.

The house itself is sagging on its foundation, giving it a depressed and defeated air. The once pristine milk-white paint is dirty and peeling off the sides. The windows are open, with stained and tattered curtains swaying whenever the wind blows. The garage door is obviously broken, as an old beat up junker of a car is parked unsteadily in the driveway. The grass is dry and dead; its brown contrasts with the beautiful, vibrant green of the neighbors'. There is no timed water system strategically nurturing the yard for maximum growth. Weeds grow haphazardly over the sidewalk and through the lawn.

And sitting on the broken porch step is a little girl: Sara. She watches girls playing down the street; her tiny fingers twist around her doll's hair absently. This doll, which is the only toy Sara cares about, looks eerily similar to the young girl, with blonde yarn hair, a pink dress, once-white lacy socks and faded Mary Jane shoes. But instead of those brilliant blue eyes—the only part of this little creature worth noting—the doll has but one black button. The other has been lost long ago.

The door opens and an older woman steps out: Sara's mother. She closes the door, squinting down the street suspiciously as a woman points her direction and says something to her friend. Sara's mother's face colors slightly, but she holds her chin

11

up high, straightens her cheap shirt, and glances at her daughter.

"Sara, get in the car."

Sara obeys silently, and her mother follows her to the junky vehicle, not bothering to lock the front door of the house. There's nothing inside worth stealing.

Sara climbs into the back. She sits the doll beside her and fastens the seatbelt with a resounding *snap*. She's big enough to sit in the front, but the car is cheap and old, and the lack of airbags keeps the young girl in the back.

After three tries, the engine reluctantly coughs itself to life. The car smells to Sara like dust from the blasting air vents (the only things in the car that actually work better than just okay), cracked leather, and, faintly, wintergreen from the air freshener that has been hanging off the rearview window since the day they pulled it out of the used car lot. That was back when her mom put on makeup and kissed her daughter goodnight.

Sara thinks back to those days and suddenly realizes that her mother no longer wears the gold wedding band on her left finger. Sara feels a twinge of sadness; she enjoyed seeing it. It was the prettiest and most expensive thing her mother ever owned. But other than feeling remorse for the lack of beauty, Sara feels nothing for the father who walked out on them long ago.

She turns her attention to their neighborhood as they drive down the street. Everyone stops to stare at their car as they pass. She doesn't care what they think, but sinks lower into her seat regardless. She peeks out at all the girls who have paused to look at them. She is slightly jealous, but she can't really miss friends; she's never had them.

"Where are we going, Mama?" Sara asks softly.

Her mother sighs. "To the doctor's. I need more pills."

Sara nods and turns away. They go to the doctor too often, but it can't be helped. Those little white pills are the only thing keeping her mother functional. Sara doesn't care to remember what it was like to eat dry cereal and ice cream those weeks her mom couldn't even try to get out of bed.

And so the car pulls out of the suburban street and onto the main road. They drive past corn fields and cows and people on bikes until they hit a small town. The town carries them, as well as the other cars, onto a bigger road with more traffic.

Sara perks up in her seat, her blue eyes sparking in excitement. To get to the city that houses her mother's long list of doctors, they have to cross the giant suspension bridge: the one with many lanes that hovers above a wide and powerful river.

The bridge is quickly coming up, and Sara squeezes her doll in excitement. The old junker merges in with the flashier cars; the business men and women chat on their cell phones, the teenagers hang out their car windows, the tourists press their faces against the glass in excitement.

Sara, too, touches her nose to the window. It is a lucky day, because her mother is in the lane closest to the edge of the bridge. As young as she is, Sara finds the water beautiful and frightening at the same time. She enjoys watching it; it is calm and swift in the center and angry and frothing around the edges. She bounces in her seat slightly, blue eyes bright, straining for a glimpse of the river.

But then they hit traffic. Her mother slaps the wheel with her palm, muttering to herself. She turns up the radio just in time to hear a news report of an accident ahead. Sara watches her mother angrily punch off the radio, letting the muted sounds from outside the closed windows bubble into their ears. Sara slumps back against the seat, knowing it will be quite a while before they get anywhere they can see the river.

As the car inches along the road, Sara nods off to sleep, the way children do. Her mother, not as unaware of her daughter as Sara may think, watches her dozing in the rearview mirror and smiles. She knows Sara gets her beauty from her father, though those lovely Maya blue eyes and that thick blonde hair are traits her mother had; their beauty wasn't nearly as obvious on her as they are on her young daughter.

And so Sara's mother looks at her daughter in the rear view mirror and loves her and wishes she could do better for her. But, instead, she reaches into her purse and pops the last white pill into her mouth. She focuses on thoughts of her ex-husband and forgets her plan to wake Sara up as they leave dry land and drive up onto the bridge. She moves the car into the detour lane, the one closest to the edge of the bridge

The car picks up speed, and so do the cars of the other drivers, keeping together as one throbbing entity, all separate extensions of a single action. Sara's hair falls into her face and her head rolls back slightly, shifting with the change in speed.

There is a sound of screeching metal, the smell of burning rubber as brakes are slammed and tires are locked against the black pavement.

Sara opens her eyes in time to see a large truck slam into the front of their car.

As soon as the cars collide, Sara's head is thrown against the window next to her. She cries out and feels as if she's falling, before the car hits the surface of the water and begins to sink.

Cold water rushes up around the windows, not finding a way in. Sara can hear her own ragged breathing; the car is suddenly filled with a deafening silence. All her young, stunned mind can take in is the silence, and how eerie it is after seven straight years of city sounds.

"Do you want to live, Sara?"

Lifting her bloodied hand away from her face, she looks at a man who's suddenly seated in the passenger's seat. His eyes are a beautiful shade of green, and they're untroubled by the situation around them. He seems simply curious and interested in her response.

Sara's head is aching, and her thinking is too slow to be normal. Her eyes shift to her mother, who is slumped over the steering wheel. She's not moving and doesn't seem to be breathing.

"Sara?"

She looks back at the man and thinks of his question. Without hesitation, she replies, "Yes."

He smiles, taking out a handkerchief and wiping a trail of blood from the side of her face. It stains the delicate material red, and he gently holds it to the wound, as a parent might to a cut on his child's cheek.

"I can save you," he continues smoothly. "There's nothing I can do for your mother, poor dear. But I got here just in time for you."

Sara's vision fills with black dots. She blinks a couple of times, to clear it, but it only seems to get worse. Her head feels like it's being split open from the inside out.

"Now, Sara, you have to tell me if you want to be saved." The man's eyes look unconcernedly out the window. "Time is of the essence, it seems."

"I want to be saved," she whispers. Her voice sounds abnormally loud in this isolated environment.

"Good!" The man smiles wider, happiness radiating from his eyes. "That's wonderful, my dear! Now all you have to do is be my marionette."

"My name isn't Mary Annette," Sara replies. She doesn't understand what he's saying, and she's not in any state to have it explained to her.

The man knows this and simply smiles kindly. "No, of course it isn't. But, you see, I have powers, Sara. I'm an immortal; surely you've heard about us on the news? No? Well, that will all change soon. But I digress! You see, I can take away all the hurt and the pain and the sadness that you will otherwise experience for the rest of your life. I can make everything better for you; doesn't that sound nice?"

Sara nods. She has already lived through so much pain and sadness in her brief lifetime, what this man is offering sounds like heaven.

The man takes his handkerchief from her head and folds it up neatly, setting it on the center console of the car. He looks around, relaxed and happy, before turning back to Sara. His green eyes show only comfort and warmth. She trusts him.

"Right, then, off we go." He holds out his hand. "Are you ready?"

Offering her mother's still body one last glance, Sara clutches her doll in one hand and reaches out with the other. She places her tiny fingers in his bigger ones. He closes his hand slowly around hers, as a Venus Fly Trap might its prey, but Sara feels only strength and warmth. She briefly wonders if this is what her father's hand might have felt like. She can hardly remember the days when he used to hold her hand.

Then, suddenly, there is horrible pain. It feels to Sara as if her entire body is being crushed from all sides by an invisible weight. She wants to cry out, but can't find her lips. She wants to thrash, to crawl away from the pain, but she can't find her limbs.

It's as if she never had a body to begin with. The pain, which she expects to dull over time, stays the same—constant, excruciating, and terrifying. Even her tiny, child's mind begins to wonder if there has ever been anything but this, if there has really been another world, or if she was awakened from a lovely dream.

Then it stops. Around Sara is dark, but a muted light seems to project from somewhere. She can't be sure if her eyes are open or not; she's forgotten how to find them.

But eventually she does. One opens first, and then the other, in a strange, uncoordinated way that seems wrong to her. She's looking at a cracked, yellowed surface with peeling paint and a musty smell.

"Welcome back." A voice greets her soothingly.

Sara blinks, but it's in that same, unfamiliar rhythm of one eye, then the other. She can't convince the rest of her body to respond; she simply sits and wonders where the voice came from, and whose voice it is.

A man appears over her. He smiles down proudly, as a child might when looking at his own pathetic artwork.

"Try to close both eyelids at the same time," he recommends. "It will be more familiar that way."

She follows his advice and finds his words to be true.

"And don't forget to breathe," he continues. "Since you can't feel anymore, you will have to form these habits, or else you might die."

Sara draws some air into her lungs, noting the expansion of her chest, the weight of the atmosphere forcing it back down again. She does this a few times and finds it easier to breathe with her mouth open.

"You'll get used to it. I'll re-teach you how to walk and move, of course, and how to remember things you'll need to be more aware of now. But for now at least, I've put you in a diaper. Since you aren't used to your body's needs any longer, it will be harder to distinguish things, like when you need to go to the bathroom." He smiles down at her.

She blinks absently. She focuses on his words and takes them in, but can't develop any feelings to go along with them. She breathes and blinks, blinks and breathes.

"Becoming my marionette meant that you lost all your emotions, bad as well as good. And not only emotions, but your sense of feeling altogether." He smiles at her.

Sara's mind processes this information. She looks at his smile; her eyes fixate on it. Smiling is meant to offer some sort of comfort. She feels nothing at all.

"Breathe," he reminds her.

She does, and then opens her mouth, her brain forming a question. Her lips move in familiar patterns, programmed into her mind, but it takes her a few tries to remember how to speak.

"Where's…Cassie?" she asks. Her speech, though perfectly clear, is halting and awkward. It sounds different to her. She realizes she's speaking in a soft monotone, with no inflection.

"Oh, your toy? It lies there, beside you."

He bends down and moves Sara's body for her, picking her up like a giant toy and setting her torso against the headboard of the bed she's lying on. Sara's head flops down as a doll's might. She

moves her eyes to see her doll and catches sight of
her hand.

"Do you like them?" the man asks eagerly.

A thick, silver string is attached to her hand. It
looks as if she were born with it, as if she was
indeed a puppet.

"I don't know," she answers. She can't seem to
like them or hate them. She's completely impassive.

"Oh, Sara, I think they're beautiful. This is
wonderful, don't you see? I've given you a gift!"
He puts his fingers under her chin and gently lifts
her face so their eyes meet. "Do you feel pain?"

Sara thinks about this. "No."

"Are you afraid?"

"No."

"Are you angry with me?" His wide green eyes
seem momentarily solemn and morose.

"No." She blinks. "I don't feel anything."

"Good! You see, the process by which I do this
is quite complex. I have to find someone willing,
someone with little hope or nothing to live for." He
smiles kindly. "I was lucky when I found you."

She stares at him blankly and takes another conscious breath.

"The longer you go without emotions, the more puppet-like you'll become. In time, you won't need to eat or drink. You'll never feel tired. I did you a favor, really. You were such a sad little girl."

"How long will I stay like this?" she asks.

A slight frown creases his brow. "Well, forever, I suppose. My puppets don't always live long. Something has gone wrong in the past; they have become no better than actual marionettes after a while. But I think I've got the solution this time, and perhaps I can keep you longer."

"I can never be changed back?"

"I have the power to change you, but why? You wanted this, didn't you?"

Sara recalls the words she spoke in the car. "Yes. I did. You're right."

"Excellent."

He lets her head down gently and goes to sit at a desk chair opposite the bed. Sara looks around as much as she can without moving her head and sees that they're in an old rundown hotel room. Only by chance and a fair amount of luck has the owner managed to keep it open.

"The only other way you can be changed is if you were to discover a soul-mate," he adds with a laugh. "But that's an extremely rare find for anyone. You can't care about love, or anything of the sort, so you're unlikely to find him. No one is *that* lucky."

Sara watches the man turn to the desk and shuffle some papers around. She searches inside herself for any sort of emotion, any hint of anything. She comes up empty, with only memories as reminder of what she has felt before. She tells herself she is sad.

But she isn't.

Part Two

Sara tilts her head up, squinting at the harsh sunlight.

"Don't stare at the sun, Sara. We talked about this," Gavis warns.

She looks back down, trying to blink the spots away from her vision. "I'm sorry, Gavis."

Gavis smiles at her, picking a box up off the curb and walking into the apartment building. He stops to talk with the building's owner, a nervous looking man with deep worry lines running across his forehead.

Sara nudges a stone off the sidewalk with her foot, creasing her brow like the owner automatically. She wonders what he's feeling right now, what kind of emotion makes his face scrunch up like that.

"Are you alright?"

She looks up to see the man watching her from the building's doorway. He squints at her, making his face even smaller.

She squints back at him.

"You seem upset," he prompts.

"You seem upset," Sara repeats.

The man glances back into the building before rubbing his forehead. He turns his attention back to Sara.

"Are you upset?" the man asks.

She rubs her forehead, as well. "Are you?"

He stares at her. She stares back. He lifts his hand to his face, shielding his eyes from the sun. Sara does the same.

His face relaxes as he smiles. "Are you copying me?"

"Of course." She smiles back.

"May I ask why?"

She drops her hand away from her face, an action all her own. She blinks at him, her expression going blank. "So I can understand."

"Understand what?" He frowns.

Sara frowns as well. "What emotions are like."

The man's eyes bug out. Sara isn't sure how to mimic that.

"Sara, don't bother the poor man," Gavis calls.

She turns her attention to him as he comes out of the building. She takes in his smile and smiles as well.

31

"Sorry, Gavis," she says.

"I-it's really no problem," the man stammers. "I just didn't believe you were telling the truth about her."

Gavis wipes his forehead, resettling the hat on his head. "I'm many things, Phillip, but a liar isn't one of them. Well, most of the time, in any case."

Sara watches Phillip frown. She frowns as well. Gavis sees her and cocks his head.

"Are you alright, Sara?" he asks.

Her eyes flick to him, her face turning neutral. "Are you?"

He smiles warmly. "I'm brilliant."

"I am as well." She grins.

"Fantastic. Would you like to help me take these things upstairs?" Gavis asks.

Sara nods, moving to take a box off the ground. She walks into the building with it, passing Phillip. He's staring at her, his face incredulous. Sara's expression copies him and stays that way until she's entered the building.

"You really shouldn't copy people so much," Gavis chides. "It makes them uncomfortable."

Sara blinks at Gavis as he walks by her, ascending a flight of stairs. "Does it make you uncomfortable?"

"Of course not. But I understand you." He smiles back at her.

She thinks about this as she follows him up to their new apartment. It's the first time that Gavis ever expressed a longing for any sort of permanent location; for ten years, they've been moving from town to town weekly, presenting their act all over the world.

Sara follows Gavis into the new apartment, looking around for the first time.

"Well?" he asks. His green eyes gleam with excitement. "What do you think?"

It's archetypal Gavis; the building is nice on the outside and horribly rundown inside. They're standing in the kitchen, where a tiny, unstable table and spindly chairs sit. To the left of her is a small living room area with an outdated television and futon. There's another door that she assumes leads to a bathroom. Everything is covered in an undisturbed layer of filth.

"It's okay," she says.

"I thought so as well."

Gavis sets his box down on the counter and moves to take the one out of her hands. "Would you like to sit on the futon and watch television?"

She tilts her head slightly. "Would I?"

"I think you would." Gavis smiles.

Sara nods, turning and walking to the next room before sitting on the couch. She picks up a small remote and turns on the machine.

×××

Sara stands on the tips of her feet, her nose pushed against the dirty window.

Go explore, Gavis had said. He rarely sent her out on her own, so she wasn't sure of where to go. She decided to explore the hallway, instead.

She presses her hand to the glass, disturbing the layer of grime. From what she can see, the town is void of all color. Everything is coated in shades of black, white and gray. Even the new pink dress Gavis bought her seems dull.

Sara drops back down onto her dirty feet, pads over the decaying floorboards, and walks to their door.

Her steps slow to a stop. She turns and looks down the staircase to the bottom floor. The light is shining through the dirty windows, washing the old wood in muted light. Sara absently twists her fingers in her dress and wonders if, by chance, she fell down these stairs, it would hurt.

She cannot feel fear or even adrenaline as she balances on the top step. She curls her delicate toes over the lip of the stair.

She stands there a while, forming her hypothesis. She's almost certain that she won't feel anything, seeing as she hasn't felt anything physical in twelve years. But she once watched a documentary about people who believed that thinking something would happen would make it happen. She wants to test out the theory for herself.

A single beam of light falls onto her feet. The silver strings glisten brightly where they melt into her practically translucent skin. She hasn't been able to tan for a long time.

Sara takes a deep breath. Breathing, like blinking, became habitual long ago. It's not something she needs

35

to remember now. And the need for food and bathroom use slowly died over time, so she no longer thinks about them.

She pulls her arms forward slightly, making the handle of her strings scrape woodenly against the floor. She bends her knees, closes her eyes and, without fear or hesitation, jumps.

Her body is thrown heavily against the banister, bashed and twisted and slammed against the stairs, the wall, the railing and, finally, the floor. It is over very quickly.

She opens her eyes. Her cheek is pressed roughly against the musty floorboards. Her arms and legs are sprawled at impossible angles and she smells the rusty scent of blood.

But she feels no pain.

She is not even uncomfortable lying on the ground. She feels nothing as a door is thrown open and feet sound on the stairs behind her.

"Sara, oh, Sara!" Gavis cries. "I heard the commotion you made! Are you alright?"

"Yes," Sara replies quietly.

"You're bleeding, and look! You've knotted your stings something terrible! I'll have to carry you to the room."

Gavis is gentle and kind as he rushes Sara back to the apartment and lays her down on the flattened futon. His fingers begin to poke at her wounds.

Sara tells herself she is upset that she feels nothing.

But she is not.

Sara tells herself that she was afraid when she fell down the stairs.

But she wasn't.

"At least your wounds aren't serious," Gavis prattles on. "I could not bear it if I lost you, Sara."

And that is true. Gavis loves her, like a child loves a plaything. He is always kind to Sara, treating her like a toy daughter. He always asks if she is comfortable, if the light is too dim, if she would enjoy watching this show or that. Sara could never care one way or the other, but she is sure she'd feel grateful, if she could.

"Did you fall?" Gavis asks.

"Yes," Sara replies dully. Technically she jumped, but there was some act of falling involved.

"There is no way I can untie these knots before the show tonight," Gavis sighs. "I'll have to pay someone to fix you."

Sara—having paid attention to Gavis' tones and expressions for years—knows he's irritated with her. She twists on the hard bed, trying to catch his eye.

"I'm sorry, Gavis," she says.

He looks up at her, a smile softening his features. "Oh, dear, I'm not angry with *you*. I should have been watching you more closely."

"I'm okay."

He sighs and stands, lifting the tan fedora off his head and running a hand through his thick hair. He starts to pace in a slow, predatory way. "I'm going to have to leave you alone more often these next few months. There are some old...colleagues of mine that I need to catch up with."

Her eyes track his movements. "I'll be fine."

"I know you will be." He sighs again, putting the hat back on. "I just feel terrible. Who will you have to talk to? You need the intellectual stimulus. You're an incredibly intelligent individual, Sara."

"I don't need people to talk to," she responds.

"That's simply because you don't *need*. I'd feel better if you had some company, that's all."

"You mean a babysitter, don't you." It isn't a question.

Her blunt tone has him wincing. "It's not that I don't trust you, Sara. It's just that... I mean, what would have happened to you if I'd been away just now? What if your injuries had been worse? You could have been seriously hurt."

She raises an eyebrow. "At least I would have died painlessly."

"Where did you learn that?" Gavis laughs. "You hardly ever use sarcasm."

"I saw it on television a few nights ago." Sara smiles.

"Wonderful!"

Sara listens to him laugh again as he walks out into the kitchen and picks up a moldy old telephone book. He leafs through the pages until he comes across the ad he's looking for. She watches him dial a cracked plastic phone. He says a few words, gives an address, and then hangs up.

He suddenly appears in front of Sara again. She looks up at his worried expression.

"I found someone to untie your strings. He'll be here soon, but I can't stay for long; the show's got to go on, you know."

"I know."

"It shouldn't take too long. It's just one giant knot really. It's preventing you from moving your hands or feet forward, which is obviously a problem."

"*Obviously.*"

Gavis' worried expression vanishes under the weight of his smile. "Sarcasm! You slay me!" He laughs some. "Would you like to watch television?"

"Sure."

Gavis turns on the old set and twists the antenna around, until he gets a station. He pounds his fist on the top until the image becomes free of snow.

The scene is of a party, with boldly dressed women and very clean men. Spotless waiters carry pristine champagne glasses filled with sparkling water on perfectly balanced trays. A band plays flawlessly at just the right decibel. Its perfection reminds Sara of the neighborhood she used to live in all those years ago.

Suddenly, the buzzer goes off. Gavis' body disappears from the spot where he was perched next to Sara and almost a second later he reappears in front of the intercom, pressing the mutilated button.

Sara is used to his magic. He uses it often when they are alone.

"Gavis' Marionettes, may I ask who's calling?" Gavis chirps politely.

"Yeah, uh, this is Mason from Sven's Repair. We unlock your locks and untie your knots?" The intercom crackles.

"I'll come down to let you in," Gavis replies cheerily.

"You could just buzz the door—" the voice suggests, too late. Gavis has already opened the door, and his body has vanished.

Sara turns her head back indifferently to watch the television.

"When a handsome man comes to call, you should always wear bright-red lipstick," one woman says to another.

"That's ridiculous," the other scoffs.

"It's the new fashion," returns the first.

Sara files this 'new fashion' away to remember for later. She has been mimicking others since the day she was turned, never feeling emotions but still copying what they look like from others.

"So she doesn't feel anything?" A voice floats up through the open apartment door.

"No, my boy. She is completely void of all emotions or physical reaction." Sara hears Gavis reply.

"That's hard to believe."

"Yes, well, don't you go trying anything funny. She is still aware of everything, even if she doesn't act in response," Gavis warns.

"Wouldn't dream of it, sir," the voice replies hastily.

Sara turns her head to see Gavis and another man appear in the room. The man looks similar to men Sara has seen on television. All those men were called handsome. Sara thinks she should have put on red lipstick.

"I have to get ready for the show, Sara," Gavis informs her. "You and Mason here will be alone for the duration. Are you okay with that?"

Sara nods. She can't care either way.

Gavis flits off to do something else. The man stands in the doorway, a bright red toolbox in his hand, staring at her. Sara looks at the toolbox for a long time, thinking that it is the most color she's seen since Gavis rented the apartment.

"Do I repulse you?" Sara asks. She sometimes has that affect on people.

"No. On the contrary I think you're—" the man stops suddenly. His face turns pink. "Uh, I mean, I'm not repulsed?"

"I'm flattered."

"Are you?"

"No."

The man stands still and continues to study Sara. She is pale with thick, pure blonde hair, gleaming blue eyes and rosy lips. She wears no expression; she simply watches him and blinks her thick lashes periodically.

"I seem to be tangled," Sara prompts him. "Some assistance?"

"Oh, yeah. Of course," he replies.

He quickly walks over and sets his toolbox on the floor by the bed. He bends down and examines her hands. She flexes her delicate fingers, causing the strings to glitter prettily. She can no longer see him, so she fixes her eyes on the broken floor boards.

"Were you always like this?" the man asks gently. He brushes his fingers against Sara's skin, which she can sense but not feel.

"No," she replies. "I was normal, once."

"Did it hurt? When this happened?"

"Very much so," she nods.

"So you remember what pain feels like?" he asks curiously.

"I remember all emotions. But that's all they are: memories."

He begins to pluck at her strings delicately. "You must be sad."

44

"I can't feel sadness."

"I would be angry at the person who robbed me of feeling, I think."

"I can't feel anger." Sara blinks.

"Do you ever get any visitors?" he asks.

"No."

"You must be lonely."

"No."

"Do you have anyone else besides that guy?" the man asks. "I mean, does anyone else live with you?"

"No."

"When was the last time you lived with someone else?"

Sara pauses to think. "Twelve years ago."

The man whistles. "And who was that?"

"My mother."

"What happened to her?"

"She died."

"I'm sorry." He seems to regret asking. Though she cannot see his face, his tone conveys sympathy and sadness.

"I'm not. But I think I would be, if I could."

"Do you miss her?"

"I can't."

"You look uncomfortable," the man remarks after a while.

Sara realizes she's hanging halfway off the couch.

"I do not feel discomfort."

"May I?" he asks, gesturing to her.

"Do what you wish," she replies.

He adjusts Sara's body so she is fully on the sofa. Her legs are now resting on the bed, and he sits down next to her.

"How old are you, Sara?"

"Nineteen," she replies. She looks back at him.

"Me, too. Hmm…" His brow furrows, and he sets back to work.

"Hmm." Sara imitates his expression.

The man seems surprised and pleased by this. "Do you know my name?"

"No."

"It's Mason."

"Mason," Sara repeats.

"Yeah," he smiles at her.

"Less chatting, more working, please." Gavis' body is suddenly in the doorway.

"Of course, sir," Mason nods. He sets back to work diligently.

"Goodbye, Sara. I am off to the show." Gavis' expression clears and he smiles at Sara.

"Goodbye, Gavis." Sara mimics his tone.

Gavis turns and disappears. It's silent for quite a long time after he disappears.

"I wouldn't worry too much about Gavis," Sara says. "He's nervous, leaving me here alone with you."

"Why?" Mason's brow furrows.

"He doesn't want anything bad to happen to me."

"I see," Mason replies. "So he loves you."

Sara cocks her head. She's never thought of it like that. "I suppose so."

"Are you two staying here long?" Mason asks uncertainly. He doesn't really know where Gavis has gone, since he did not hear him leave. Despite Sara's reassurances, he's wary of Gavis.

"I don't know. Perhaps," Sara shrugs.

Suddenly, Sara's arm jerks back. Mason has pulled too roughly on the string connected to her hand.

"Sorry!" Mason blurts. "I didn't mean to hurt you."

"You didn't. I cannot feel physical pain." Sara looks over her shoulder at him.

He studies her quietly for a long period of time.

"Do you feel anything physical?" he asks.

"No. It took me a long time to adjust to moving without feeling the movement." Sara wiggles her fingers.

Mason still stares at her, shaking his head slowly. "I really can't wrap my head around it."

"It's not so terrible. I cannot feel sadness or anger or pain. Does that truly sound awful?" she asks.

"But I think the loss of good feelings would cancel out the lack of bad ones," Mason argues.

"I don't miss good emotions."

"That's worse than anything."

They are quiet for a long time. Finally, Mason finds another question to ask.

"How did you get yourself tangled?"

"I threw myself down the stairs. I wanted to see if I could hurt," she answers serenely.

"That's awful!" Mason is appalled.

"Not really. I felt nothing. Nothing physical, remember?"

"Still…" Mason's expression is conflicted.

Sara senses that she has said something wrong. She tries to move onto another subject.

"I can remember them, though," Sara thinks aloud. "They are stronger than the memory of good emotions, but I think it's enough to remember."

"Why are your bad memories stronger than good?" he asks.

"I was an unhappy child. Gavis offered me this life when I was in a hopeless and futile situation. I would be dead if not for him," Sara informs him.

"What happened?"

Sara starts talking. She tells him everything about her childhood; about her depressed mother, her father that left them long ago and her little pathetic life. She tells him about the day of the car accident, and how

49

Gavis came to her rescue, like a hero in a nice suit and Gucci shoes.

And she continues. She tells Mason all about waking up and not feeling, about knowing that each year a little more of her would evaporate. She tells him about being able to stop eating and stop sleeping, about being stared at and being alone. She tells him about Gavis' promise that she would never feel anything again unless he changed her or she found her soul mate.

After she is done, Mason is quiet. She senses him plucking at her strings with great care.

She turns back to him, studying his expression. She notices his eyes flit around the room, just once, as if he is taking in his surroundings. A wry smile touches his lips. Sara feels that it has been quiet for too long.

"You have run out of questions," Sara notes.

"Do my questions bother you?"

His laugh makes her smile reflexively. "I am not bothered by anything."

"Tell me something you like," Mason prompts.

"I cannot like things, Mason. I seem to be repeating myself." She looks away.

"Well you must have *liked* something."

"I have a doll from my childhood still," Sara informs him.

Sara turns and kicks her foot in the direction of a closet. The door is crooked on its hinges, but Mason goes over and opens it, peering into the darkness.

He pulls the doll out of the darkness. "Why is she stuffed in there?"

"So I can be with her when Gavis sleeps." Sara watches him. Her younger self would have been nervous of her doll in a stranger's hands.

"So why is she in here?" Mason repeats.

"I don't sleep anymore. Since this is the only room, Gavis sleeps here and there's nowhere else to go. So I stay in the closet, out of the way," she explains.

"You stand in there?" Mason is shocked.

"I have to hang my strings up every night so they won't tangle," she says matter-of-factly.

"You shouldn't be locked in a closet."

"Why not?" Sara asks blandly. She does not understand his outrage.

"Because you are a human! Humans do not deserve to be locked up in the dark!"

"Am I human?" She pauses. "What makes one human? I always assumed that emotions were what made up a person's humanity. Of course, animals can get angry and upset, but they don't feel as much as humans. The television says that their brains do not have the capacity. With the absence of emotions, I get more wooden every year. I need not sleep, drink or eat. I feel no hunger, and I never feel tired. Does that sound human to you?"

She is stating everything she has thought to herself over the past ten years, without feeling or inflection. It is almost painful for Mason to hear her talk without passion or variety.

"But you still have the power to make your own choices!" Mason cries. "John Locke stated that the actions and decisions of humans set them apart from other creatures. That the freedom to open a door and walk outside or paint a picture is what makes us human."

"There is a robot in China that can complete those actions," Sara counters. "Dale Carnegie, American lecturer and author, once said, 'When dealing with people, remember that you are not dealing with creatures of logic, but creatures of emotion.'"

Mason's brow furrows. He looks down at the little doll he has been cradling inadvertently in his hand. With him standing in a sliver of light seeping in through the dirty window, Sara can see him clearly. Mason's clothes are wrinkled and his hair is mussed, but his face and arms are clean. Sara looks down at her own dirty skin.

Something inside her seems to shift. She can't tell what it is, but she knows it is important. She senses that she is off balance, but when she shifts on the bed, she finds her position quite solid.

"Leo Nikolayevich Tolstoy, Russian moral thinker, novelist and philosopher once said 'The sole meaning in life is to serve humanity,'" Mason says slowly.

"How do you know so much about philosophers?" Sara questions.

She still senses something is off. She tries to ignore it.

"I read a lot," Mason replies. He seems somewhat embarrassed now. "What about you?"

"I watch the television and read whatever Gavis has lying around," Sara replies.

"Oh," Mason lets it drop. "Anyway, back to the quote. What does it mean to you?"

"Will you repeat it?" Sara asks.

Mason does. Sara thinks for a long time.

"I think he meant that if someone can do nothing for her fellow humans, then she's not human," Sara shrugs. "You picked a bad example to solidify your side of the argument."

"You're a very technical thinker," Mason remarks.

Sara cannot tell if this is rhetorical, or if she is supposed to answer. She chooses to say something, regardless. "You have the ability to put emotion into your thoughts. I am unable to do so."

Mason doesn't respond. Sara can tell that he is thinking quite hard, but she doesn't know what it is, yet. She waits for him to speak.

"Sara, what do you live for?" Mason asks suddenly.

"I don't understand the question." She shakes her head. "I am alive because I was born and survived into adulthood."

"No, no. That's not what I mean." Mason crosses over to her and sets the doll on the bed. "I live because I make money to help take care of my family. I live to see my friends smiling and happy. I live because I believe that one day I'll fall in love with a girl and we'll get married and have a family of our own. I live for the past I've survived, I live for the present and I live for the future. What do *you* live for?"

Sara looks up into his face, full of solemn passion. She thinks about what he has just said and she compares her own existence with what he is suggesting.

"I live because I once felt. I cannot care about my future, although I spend a great deal of time remembering my past."

"But take Tolstoy's quote into account. You're a logical thinker. Think about this logically," he encourages. He sets back to work untying her knots.

"Are you suggesting that if I do something to help fellow humans and give my life meaning, I will revert back to my human form?" Sara asks.

"I think that could help you get back your emotions." He pauses. "Sara, I barely know you, but from what I can see, you're really smart. Your brain works almost like a computer's. So why haven't you figured this out before?"

"I have no motivation to find my emotions. I have no drive to find them, nor can I miss them," she explains. "Besides, I think your hypothesis is wrong."

"Why?" Mason demands.

"Because what can I possibly do for someone else that would give my life meaning?" She asks. "If I collected money for the poor, I could not care about them. If I helped a lost child find its way home, my existence would not be altered."

"I see your point," Mason admits. "But there must be something. Something that that guy—uh, Gavis—isn't telling you."

They are quiet for a long time.

Sara goes on thinking about Mason's words. Her brain is more active than it has been in years, but she doesn't understand why she is thinking so much in this moment. It is almost as if Mason makes her... *want* to feel.

But she has always wanted to feel, hasn't she? She threw herself down those stairs as an experiment; she tells herself she is feeling something because she knows that she is supposed to. She is trying to be human. She has always been trying to be human.

She feels the shift happening inside her again. She flops onto her back, surprising Mason. She tells him everything she has just discovered, even the shift.

"So you feel want?" Mason asks. He's clearly excited by this discovery.

"I don't so much as feel it as it just happens. Like a habit one cannot break. That's what Gavis told me was the reason I keep my doll. It's simply a habit from when I once felt."

"So do you think your wanting to be human is habitual or just one emotion that slipped through the cracks when you were turned?" Mason questions.

"I don't know. Gavis told me about other girls he turned. He told me that they each retained a particular emotion from their human-stage."

"There were other girls? What happened to them? Why just one emotion? How was that emotion determined?" Mason blurts.

"Yes, there were others. They eventually turned into regular puppets. They went without feeling for so long they turned into something not human. Gavis still has them, but he won't let me see them. That's who he took to the show tonight. The audience will be disappointed that they aren't alive but will be entertained nonetheless. As for your other questions, it was always just one emotion, maybe the last emotion the girl felt, or the one she felt most often," Sara replies.

"Will you turn into a non-living puppet? Does your emotion of want fit in the description of the other girls?"

"I will, eventually. Turn into a puppet, I mean. And yes, wanting things was something I always felt. I never knew what was wrong with my mother but looking back on it now, I can determine that she was quite depressed. We never had much, although we lived in a nice neighborhood."

"How did your mother manage to keep the house?" Mason asks.

"My father left when I was very, very small. He sent checks to pay the mortgage, the water, the electricity. But that was it," Sara clarifies.

"What was your last emotion?" Mason asks.

Sara closes her eyes and thinks hard for a few seconds. "I remember the fear... sorrow, because my mother was dead... pain, from hitting my head on the window... and want."

"What did you want?"

Sara opens her eyes and meets Mason's gaze. "I wanted what Gavis was offering; escape from pain."

"But that proves my earlier point!" Mason exclaims. "If you want to help someone then you can unlock the key to your emotions."

"I don't think that's right," Sara frowns. "It doesn't make any sense."

"Ah, here we go." With a final tug of her strings, the knots fall apart.

59

Sara sits up and rubs her arms mechanically. They are stiff from being tied so long. She does not exactly feel the stiffness, but she senses it.

"What do you think the shift means?" Mason asks.

"Why do you care so much? You don't even know me," Sara says, looking at him.

"I… I honestly have no idea. But this is right. I feel that I should help you. I *want* to help you." Mason's expression is confused, but his words are honest.

"I still do not understand your drive to help. Do you feel that way for everyone? Is that it?" Sara inquires.

"No, actually. I'm usually pretty selfish," Mason replies smoothly.

She watches his face. After a few moments, she says, "You're lying."

He's obviously surprised. "What makes you say that?"

"I can tell when people are lying. Gavis taught me how to read people's facial expressions and body language, so that nothing bad would happen to me for not being suspicious." She tilts her head. "I know you're lying."

"Enough about me," he replies quickly. He's suddenly very nervous. "I have some more questions. I've seen you smile. Why do you do that, if you can't feel the emotion that drives it? Is it just a habit?"

"No, it's not a habit. I mostly just copy other people. I could tell that you were happy, so I copied that emotion."

"So you just copy others?" he asks.

"Not always. Sometimes people explain to me how they feel."

"Like when?"

She thinks about this some, wondering how best to explain it to him. She suddenly gets an idea. Reaching out, she places her hand on the side of Mason's face.

His charismatic smile immediately disappears. He watches her seriously, his breath catching in his throat. He says nothing, only waits, frozen.

Sara notes all his facial reactions. Even though she cannot feel his skin, she can sense that they're touching. She notes how his pupils dilate, how his eyes seem surprised and something else she can't identify. She wonders if her body can still react just as physically.

"Like now," Sara says quietly. "Mason, what do you feel right now?"

He says nothing for a long time. He reaches up and holds her wrist, squeezing it gently. Sara can see it, sense it, but still cannot feel it. This would disappoint her, if she could feel. She finds herself wanting to touch this boy and actually feel him.

"I can't answer your question." Mason swallows hard.

"Why?"

"Because, Sara. You can't understand."

"Help me to."

"I can't."

"Please?"

"No. I'm telling you. I can't." He pulls away from her, his actions gentler than his tone.

Sara's hand drops to the bed. She flexes her fingers, sensing the absence of heat. She presses her hand to her face, trying to feel the temperature difference. She realizes that she can, but just faintly.

So faintly, in fact, that she decides she is just making it up. Her hand falls from her cheek, although she still looks at Mason.

"You have helped me a lot tonight," she says steadily. "Thank you."

"You're welcome," he smiles. The gesture seems forced, more than a little troubled.

"I should stay away from you," he says. "If I make Gavis angry, he could kill me. They do, sometimes. They kill people with their powers."

"Gavis wouldn't hurt you." Sara shakes her head. "He is odd, but he is not a danger."

"I did my job. I should go home," Mason continues.

"Then go," Sara tucks her feet under her dress. "It doesn't bother me if you stay or not."

Sara turns back to the television. She is watching something from the late 1960's, something her mother would have liked. Mason sits quietly beside her for a few seconds.

"I would like to see you again," he says slowly.

"If I'm not here, I'll be at the garden show," Sara replies.

"Would Gavis mind?" Mason flinches as though the thought of Gavis minding *anything* he did was painful.

"Probably not. Gavis lets me do what I want," Sara repeats.

"Do you want to see me again?" Mason asks. He seems slightly nervous.

"You could be useful in the recovery of my emotions," Sara looks at him from the corner of her eye. "And you're good for stimulating conversations."

Mason hesitates, put off by her indifferent words. "Is that a yes?"

"It's a yes."

"Alright."

Mason sits awkwardly on the bed for a few more seconds before clearing his throat.

"I'll be going, then," he says hesitantly.

He gets up, takes his toolbox and pauses before leaving the room.

Sara waits until his hand is on the front door knob before calling after him, "Goodbye, Mason."

"Goodbye, Sara," Mason smiles at the door before slipping through it and closing it gently.

Part Three

Gavis watches the young man leave the apartment building. Wrapped in shadows, he waits as the boy walks away. He hesitates and then begins to follow the kid down the darkened street.

The boy seems ordinary. Gavis assesses the dark eyes, the hair that's just a few shades lighter, the tall, lean frame. The kid is simply that: a kid. But unlike the cocky snots walking around these days, this one seems a bit different. Like there's something off about him.

Gavis' talents stretch far beyond warping emotions. He also influences the way people feel at any given time and can tell what they're thinking simply by checking out their emotions. He has killed people simply by convincing them that they're in intense pain. He sees the bonds between people, so he knows if a boy thinks the girl he's talking to is a selfish airhead. Anyone else would see best friends having normal interactions. He can jump through time and make himself invisible.

He has another, more random ability: he can change the colors of objects to whatever he pleases. He knew a girl long ago who had the ability to grow flowers with the wave of her hand. She, too, could change the colors of things, and loved to create unnaturally blue flowers. He remembers her fondly and wonders what she would think of him if she could see him now—creeping up on a stranger.

Gavis walks behind the boy, keeping his own body unseen. Perhaps it's the fact he hasn't had a permanent home in years, or maybe it's his natural paranoia kicking in, but he feels uneasy.

Something about Mason unsettles Gavis. It could be the way the boy carries himself, the untapped intelligence, the sharpness of his eyes. He could hurt Gavis.

Gavis starts to probe Mason's mind. He's looking for something specific, anything that would validate his suspicion that this boy is a threat not only to himself, but to Sara as well. Mainly, to Sara's condition.

He skims the surface but doesn't catch anything alarming. He digs a little deeper, just to be safe. What he finds feels to him like he has run into a brick wall or swallowed rocks. It knots his stomach and gives him a massive headache.

Gavis curses his own name, wishing he'd never rented out that blasted apartment. In any other city they would have been safe, he and Sara. Because here he is: Sara's other half; her soul mate. Gavis' best doll about to be freed by a boy who is none the wiser. A child, about to take Gavis' most prized possession.

Gavis influences people and feels no regret; he got over his feeble conscience about four thousand years ago. He realized pretty early on that he couldn't be a nice person and survive.

And he reminds himself of that as he pulls on the brim of his fedora and influences Mason's emotions toward Sara. He finds that tiny, undeveloped bond and crushes it. He does everything he can think of to destroy it.

But he can't seem to change it at all. He can't even make the boy feel a *little* disinterested in Sara. Frustrated, he peers into the kid's face. Mason is smiling slightly, a faraway look on his face. Gavis can feel the turmoil in the young man's stomach, the confusion overwhelming his heart. Mason's completely oblivious to the power walking unseen and unheard beside him.

"It seems I have underestimated the control of a bond," Gavis whispers to Mason. The pain in Gavis' skull increases. "I will just have to find other ways to keep you from her. But now I wonder what disobedient thoughts you have planted in her head…"

Mason ducks quickly into his building. Gavis pauses for a second. He knows he's many unpleasant things, but an intruder he is *not*. His curiosity wins out over his hesitation, however, and he darts in before the door can fully close.

On the outside, the house looks much older than it is. The bricks are worn down, discolored. The house itself is slowly sinking into the ground. This young man's family clearly lives from paycheck to paycheck, with little left over.

A voice rings out from another room. "Mason? Is that you, son?"

"It's me, Ma," he calls back.

His voice shows none of the worry he has been feeling the whole trip home. He seems almost too

71

enthusiastic. Gavis looks at him, quietly wondering what could have brought on this brave face.

Mason sets his toolbox on a table in the hall. He kicks off his boots and places them neatly next to about a dozen other pairs of all sizes.

There's a sound of tiny feet pounding on the floor above, and then children come sprinting down the stairs, oldest ones first. They start shouting as soon as they see Mason.

"Mason's home!"

"Mason!"

"He's back!"

Mason bends down to scoop up a little girl, laughing as the other children jump up on him like overly-excited puppies.

Gavis watches with interest. He has never seen a teenager so tolerant of younger siblings, especially one with the feelings Mason has chewing away at his gut.

"Mason, I could use your help," the voice from the kitchen calls again.

Mason's face turns towards the sound. His smile dies down a little, but he seems to force it back on. He

72

turns his attention back to the younger kids. "You guys go upstairs, okay? Ma's got enough to deal with right now."

"But Mary, Lisa, and Josephine are in the kitchen. You can come and play with us," the girl in his arms pleads, throwing her arms around his neck.

"Later," Mason promises. He sets her down before shooing the others back up the stairs.

They gather together on the stair case, wrapping their hands around the bars as if they were prisoners. Several of the boys dangle over the top, looking down at their older brother. Curious, Gavis searches the emotions of the children. Most of them are old enough to project their feelings; they all radiate love for the eldest child. The older boys particularly swell with pride and admiration. Confused, Gavis wonders why they feel this way towards Mason. Those emotions are normally reserved for the man of the house: the father.

Mason walks through the doorway at the end of the hallway. Gavis trails after him, absorbed in the curling wallpaper on the walls and faded paint on the banister. He finds himself following Mason into the kitchen.

Three girls are standing at a counter, sleeves rolled up past their elbows. Their arms are covered in flour and they knead dough steadily. An older woman is cutting up vegetables, with her eye on a pot of water on the stove that's almost boiling.

"Hello, Mason!" the younger girls chorus.

"Lisa, Mary, Josephine." He nods at each of them in turn.

The girls beam at him. To Gavis, they look tired—too tired for young teenage girls. They wear no makeup, or expensive clothes. Their hair is pulled back from their faces in sloppy ponytails, and their faces are streaked with flour.

"Hello, son. How was work?" His mother smiles thinly at him. She looks more exhausted then all the others put together.

"Fine, Ma. I didn't get paid yet, but I will tomorrow. Sven will have the money for me then." Mason shrugs slightly. He crosses the small kitchen and plants a kiss on his mother's worn cheek.

"That's fine, dear," she replies. Gavis can sense the unease that coils through her. She obviously doesn't like it when Mason returns home without the day's pay.

"What am I doing?" Mason asks. He pushes his sleeves up on his biceps.

His mother hands him the knife and gestures at some vegetables. "Cutting these."

"Excellent." He sets to work without complaint.

Gavis reaches out to Mason's feelings. The boy's focused on not cutting himself, but he is also thinking of Sara. Gavis feels a wave of possessiveness, but he lets it go, for now.

"How was work?" Mason asks the sister closest to him.

"Fine," she replies. "I got to cover Lucy's shift, so I brought home double the tips."

"You tired?"

"Yeah," she murmurs quietly. She looks a little embarrassed.

They're quiet for a little while before Mason says, "I'll clear up after dinner. You need to get some sleep. To, you know, keep your grades up."

"Thanks, Mason." She smiles wearily.

"Yeah."

Gavis senses her gratitude through his pounding head. His migraines always worsen when he uses his powers. He ignores it. He is used to headaches when he over exerts himself. He decides he'd better go before it gets any worse. He's seen enough, anyway.

Gavis leaves the house, thinking that the boy's kindness will most likely be his downfall.

×××

The music fills the theater, echoing into the unused balcony and evaporating in the rafters.

Sara spins slowly, balancing on the toes of one foot. Her arms bow out gracefully. Of course, she isn't the one moving her body; Gavis is.

The people in the crowd murmur pleasantly. They think she's striking. Like a doll… a living doll. She catches sight of some of their faces. Men and women, with one or two little children in the front row. They sit in awe of her. She ignores their gawking faces and concentrates on smiling softly and mysteriously, just like Gavis taught her.

The song drifts to an end. Her body slows to a stop. She holds that position until the curtains close. From what she can see, the crowd is on its feet, roaring enthusiasm for her intricate dance.

"Was that alright, Gavis?" she asks indifferently.

"Perfect, Sara, perfect." Gavis beams down at her. He's balancing on the rafters. After a beat, he drops her handle and materializes beside her, daintily catching the wood before it clatters to the ground.

Sara watches the strings shrink back to their normal size. Gavis has always been able to stretch them out to fit the height of the stage. She is used to it by now.

"You have something to tell me?" Gavis prompts. He's felt her mind working hard the entire night.

"I found an emotion," she says.

"Oh?" He turns away, disinterested.

Sara trails along after him. "It's want."

"Well, I always knew that. You just hadn't figured it out," Gavis shrugs.

"Why didn't you tell me?" Sara asks.

"It just… never came up." Gavis smiles at her. "Besides, you know now, so what harm have I done?"

Sara blinks, and reasons through it. He has lied through omission, but it hasn't actually hurt her. Unable to get angry at him anyway, she quickly forgets the incident.

Her dress—currently a dark shade of blue—melts back to its usual pink. Sara smoothes the fabric, waiting until the color is completely returned before following Gavis.

"I'm going to see Mason tonight," she continues.

"Mason?" Gavis stalks out into the hall of the theater.

"The boy from Sven's Repair," Sara replies.

"Oh, right. Him." Gavis makes a face when Sara isn't looking. "Why him?"

"Because I want to." Sara pulls her hair out of its tight bun. "Because I have the ability to do what I want."

Gavis chuckles warmly. "You sound so much like a *normal* teenager,"

"I don't understand your tone, so I will take that as a compliment. Thank you, Gavis," Sara replies mechanically.

"What makes you think Mason wants to see you?" Gavis sighs.

"Well, I did come to the show tonight."

Gavis stiffens before slowly turning around. Mason stands there, with a self conscious half-smile on his face. He's dressed in stiff looking clothes, clearly trying to blend in more with the crowd. To Gavis he just looks sloppy. The boy's tie is loosened, his slacks are creased, his shirt is wrinkled. Gavis notes the boy's checkered Converse Chucks with disdain. Gavis' own slate gray suit and fedora— with a red tie to match the feather in his hat—seems to intimidate the boy. It shows him just a snippet of Gavis' extensive life. Mason's features are relaxed, but Gavis can sense the tension inside of him.

"Hello, Mason," Sara chirps politely.

"Hello, Sara." Mason dips his head in her direction.

Gavis levels a glare at Mason.

"Please, Gavis?" Sara asks.

"I'll have her home before eleven, sir. I'll make sure she stays safe," Mason promises.

Gavis' eyes narrow. "You realize she can never like you. I don't know what kind of game you're playing, boy, but I told you before. She doesn't feel anything. She can't ever like you back or want to get physical with you."

"It's, uh, it's not that way. I just enjoy talking to her." Mason's face turns red. "She's, you know… different."

"Yes, she's different alright," Gavis growls.

"Gavis, I want to go," Sara interrupts. She can't understand why Gavis is being so hostile. "I *want* to."

Gavis bristles for a few more seconds before reluctantly relaxing. He tugs at his lapels, straightening his suit. He can't see any harm in letting the two be together. The bond between them won't become a problem for a long time yet, and it's what Sara wants…"Fine."

"Thank you, Gavis." Sara smiles.

"Thank you, sir." Mason is obviously relieved.

Gavis turns and stalks away. "Have her home by eleven."

"Will do," Mason calls.

Sara tugs on Mason's sleeve. She waits until he looks down at her before speaking. "Where are we going?"

"I was thinking the park," he replies. "Is that somewhere you'd want to go?"

"I think so." She smiles.

He smiles back. "Excellent."

×××

The park is… well, what is it?

Sara can't find any words to describe it. Beautiful? That can't be, because her logical mind cannot discern beauty. Impressive? She cannot be impressed. Amazing? What does that word even mean?

"Mason, what does amazing mean?" she asks.

Mason looks up at her, pulled from his own thoughts. "It… I'm not sure, actually. You say something's amazing when you like it a lot. Or when you're impressed by something you can be amazed."

"Would you say that this park is amazing?" she continues.

Mason follows her with his eyes as she steps onto a park bench, extending her arms for balance. He fights

81

his instinctual repulsion the sight of her strings stirs in him. He tries to keep his expression smooth as her wooden handle clunks against the side of the bench.

"Mason?" Sara prompts.

He shakes himself slightly. "It's okay, I guess."

"I think I would find it amazing," she tells him.

Sara watches as Mason lies back in the grass, eyes trained on the sky. She glances upwards, trying to see what he is looking at.

"What are you doing?" Sara asks.

"Looking for stars. You've never done that?" Mason puts his hands behind his head, looking over at her.

"No. What's it like?" Sara drops her hands, looking down at him.

"Calming, I guess. You can't really see them tonight, though."

Sara tilts her head up towards the sky. She can feel Mason's eyes on her.

"I can't understand the appeal," she finally says.

"Come and lie on the grass. It's better that way," he assures her.

Sara hops off the bench and her string gets caught between two of the wooden slats. She tries to tug it out unsuccessfully before going back and unhooking it. She turns back and takes a few steps over to the grass, sinking down beside Mason. She mimics him, lying back and looking up at the sky.

She starts to think about the grass and how she can't recognize if it's cold outside. She waits for a few minutes, to see if Mason will say anything. When he doesn't, Sara wriggles closer to him. He looks at her, startled, before she tucks herself into his side.

"Is it cold out here?" Sara asks.

"Well, yeah, I guess," Mason replies.

Sara slips her hand inside Mason's open jacket, tucking her fingers around his middle. She waits to see if the temperature will change and if she will be able to feel it. She closes her eyes and concentrates.

"You're warm," she finally comments.

"You can feel that?" he asks.

"I think so. I noted that I could, when I touched your face the last time. But I couldn't tell the difference between warmth and cold before I touched you." She frowns. "I can't really tell anyway. I'm only noticing a very slight difference."

"That's strange. What do you think it means?" he asks.

"I'm not sure," she replies.

The temperature difference Sara feels wouldn't be discernable to any normal person. But she's gone so long without feeling anything, it's almost like the air has plummeted twenty degrees. She shivers.

"It's cold," she says.

Mason smiles. "Sit up a sec."

She moves away from him, taking one of her strings into her fingers and playing with it. He sits up, shrugs out of his jacket, and gently places it around her shoulders. He flops down on the cool grass, placing one arm across his stomach and flinging the other carelessly from his body; it's a subtle invitation for her to lay back in the dip of his shoulder.

Sara pulls the leather jacket closer around herself, straining to feel any sort of temperature difference. She thinks she can, but just barely. She doesn't let it go this time, but files the information away for later. She won't forget.

"Better?" Mason asks.

"Yes, thank you."

She lies back down, pressing close to him. She wants to feel as much as she can with this boy. She views him differently than Gavis; Mason's less of a father figure and more of a friend. She knows she's supposed to feel the difference between the two, but she can't.

They're quiet for a long time, and Sara memorizes the patterns she can hear in Mason's body: his steady heartbeat, the rhythmic up-and-down of his breathing. She holds her breath for a second and then lets it out, making sure to keep her breaths in time with his.

"Can I ask you something?" Mason says finally.

"Of course."

"What happened to your father?"

Sara shifts her head back to see his face. She watches him lift a hand to brush away some stray hair off his forehead. His eyes widen, and he drops his fist to his side.

85

"I assume he left my mother. I was never told. I know he paid our bills, but that's about it. He could have another family somewhere, I guess. Or he could be dead," Sara replies.

She watches his expression darken before he turns his eyes to the sky. "My father died."

"How did he die?" she asks.

She didn't question Mason's behavior before, but now she's perplexed. He refuses to look at her, though they're quite close and it would be easier to. He also doesn't answer right away. He presses his lips together so they pale slightly.

"He had a heart attack. It wasn't unexpected. He was overworked and underpaid. It happens, I guess," he answers finally.

"Do you miss him?" she asks. Perhaps his sorrow is the reason he won't meet her gaze.

"I miss his paycheck. When he wasn't working, he was getting drunk." He stops to take a deep breath. "When he got drunk, he hit me or my ma."

"That's terrible," Sara says. She can sort of understand Mason's discomfort. "Did you feel powerless?"

"What?" Mason asks.

He does look at her now, startled, and his lips accidentally brush her forehead. He jerks back slightly, his face turning red.

"When your father hit your mother, did you feel powerless?" Sara continues.

She does not interpret the brush of his mouth on her face as romantic. She knows he was unsure of their proximity, and the touch was merely accidental. She dismisses it.

"Yeah, how did you—"

"I read once that most children, particularly males, feel powerless in an abusive situation," Sara interrupts. "They feel guilty that they hadn't been able to stop it, especially if they weren't the only ones abused. I was wondering if you felt the same way."

"Oh." Mason looks away again.

They're quiet for a while. Mason stares at the sky and Sara stares at Mason. She checks to make sure they're breathing in sync before she decides to ask a question.

"Why do you look away when we talk?"

Mason meets her gaze, careful of their closeness this time. "What?"

"When you and I talk, you avoid my gaze. I was wondering why that is," she elaborates.

"I just feel…uncomfortable, I guess."

"Why?"

"I don't like thinking about my father," Mason replies.

"And that causes you to look away?" Sara presses.

"Well, yeah, I guess. I've just never told anyone about the… abuse," he confesses.

"Is it a secret?" Sara stage-whispers.

Mason's mouth twitches up at the corner. "I dunno. I guess."

"You told me a secret?" Sara smiles.

"I guess I did, yeah." His brow quirks up. "How does that make you feel?"

"Happy."

"Really?"

"No."

Mason laughs before carefully removing his arm from under her head. He sits up, bends one leg, rests his elbow on it and runs a hand through his hair. He stares out at the pond opposite from them.

Once again, Sara does not understand Mason's reaction. Why did he pull away from her? Did she say something wrong? She curls up inside his jacket, breathing in his scent. She starts to run their conversation through her head. She begins to feel colder.

"I think you are the key," Sara announces quietly.

Mason looks back at her. "The key?"

"My key. The secret to unlocking my emotions. Aside from the fact I feel temperature differences when I'm around you, Gavis seems threatened by you. He says your name disdainfully and he was reluctant to let me go tonight. I think you can help me."

She waits for him to say something. She keeps her eyes trained on Mason's still form. He doesn't look at her.

Finally, he blows out a breath. "I think I'd better take you home."

He pulls Sara to her feet and Sara can't help but notice him looking at her—*really* looking. She wants to like this; she wants his attention on her. But most of all, she wants to see him again.

They walk together in silence. After a while, Sara wraps her strings around her hands several times, to get her handle up off the ground.

She notices that Mason seems sure of his steps, as if he knows this part of town well. He puts his arm around Sara's shoulders gently. She presses closer to him, to feel his warmth. She wants to take pleasure in the moment.

Mason is still deep in thought when they approach Sara's building. They stand there for a moment, facing each other. Mason's eyes are on the ground and Sara's eyes are on Mason. She shivers a little in his jacket.

"You can kiss me, if you want," she says.

Mason's gaze snaps up to hers. "What?"

"You can kiss me, if you want," she repeats a little louder.

He's quiet for a long time, just staring at her. "I can't," he says finally.

She shakes her head. "Yes, you could."

"No, I mean...I just can't, Sara. I'm sorry."

"Okay." She shrugs out of his jacket indifferently. "Will I see you tomorrow?"

"I-I have to work."

She notices his sudden unease. His eyes roam the street, refusing to rest on her. She calls his attention back to her, "The next day?"

Mason pulls his jacket out of her hands and takes another step away. She watches as his eyes turn up toward her building. They focus on something up high; she watches his skin color pale.

Wanting to know what has his attention, she twists around to look. She sees nothing but a muted light coming from a top floor window. She realizes it's muted because someone's standing in front of it: Gavis. She can't make out Gavis' expression because his fedora is pulled too low over his face.

"Probably not, Sara," Mason replies grudgingly.

"I want to see you again." She doesn't want him to go.

"You will… just not for a while." Mason steps out onto the deserted road, backing to the other side.

His eyes stay on Sara's window, and she doesn't want this. She wants him to look at her like he did earlier. She wants to make him look at her like that.

"Do you want to see me, Mason?" Sara asks.

She watches as a muscle in his jaw works. He's quiet for a few seconds before his eyes drop to hers. "Of course I do, Sara. I'll always want to see you."

"Goodbye, then." Satisfied, Sara turns to leave.

She opens the door and walks in without a second glance. Gavis appears and catches the door before it closes. She blinks at him.

"Go upstairs, Sara," he growls.

She watches as he takes a few steps out onto the sidewalk, stopping to watch the boy from under his expensive hat. Sara doesn't want to go upstairs, now that Gavis is outside with Mason. But she follows Gavis' order anyway, wondering what she'll be able to see from the window.

Meanwhile, the two men stand at opposite sides of the street, staring at each other. Gavis watches Mason palm his horribly tacky jacket in one hand, and tries to stop himself from sneering. He feels the boy struggling with all the emotions crashing inside of him.

"I will save her. I don't know how, but I will," Mason says.

Gavis resists the urge to laugh knowingly. The boy is surprised by his own forceful tone. He knows nothing of his own feelings, and, beautifully, even less about Gavis. Gavis smiles slowly, showing the boy that he's not threatened by him. He vanishes right before Mason's eyes.

As expected, the boy jerks up, his muscles locking like those of a startled animal. His wild eyes strain the dark for any sign of Gavis, even though he continues to stand in the same spot. Gavis allows himself a victorious smile.

The boy finally seems to convince himself to move. He starts to back down the deserted street, his eyes scrutinizing the place where Gavis stands.

"Good luck," Gavis calls out darkly. Predictably, the coward turns and sprints down the street, to get as far away from Gavis—and Sara—as he possibly can.

Gavis reappears, resettles the fedora on his head, and turns back to the building, a pleased smile resting on his lips.

×××

Sara floats through the apartment, letting her handle clank roughly against the floor. She is restless and, of course, she's aware of a set of eyes watching her.

Gavis is still celebrating his small victory. He managed to scare the boy away four days ago, but he's still unsure about how this might pan out for himself. For the umpteenth time, he checks Sara's bond.

It's dramatically stronger. He still regrets letting the two alone together, but he hadn't fathomed that such a change could occur. She has to be aware of it by now, but she hasn't said anything to Gavis. This upsets him, because Sara always tells him everything she observes about herself and the things around her. He senses her emotions shift back to want and he feels slightly threatened.

"What about the boy?" he asks.

Sara looks over at him. "I want to see him."

"He doesn't want to see you." Gavis says levelly. A bubble of anger forms in his chest.

"He said we'd see each other again," Sara argues.

"He lied."

"He did not." Sara rounds on Gavis; her eyes narrow.

Gavis is surprised. Sara has never disagreed or shown any kind of hostility towards him before. "You can't be sure."

"I *am* sure." Sara turns and ghosts into the bathroom, placid once more.

Gavis sits in his own shock, turning his eyes to the window. Sara's emotions are resurfacing, even if she doesn't realize it yet. Her defiance is just a faint shadow, but it's there. Gavis takes comfort in the fact that since Mason has left, the shadows are receding. It seems that when she is away from the boy, she returns to her normal state.

He starts to remember the way she was directly after the few hours she spent with him. Bright eyed, chatter filled, smiling. Color showed in her cheeks. Gavis shudders at the memory, pushing it back into a corner of his mind.

The clock chimes. Gavis turns his attention to it, reminded that he has an appointment with a real estate agent two towns over. He also has another engagement. This will take much longer.

"Sara? I'm going out for a few days," he calls.

"Okay. I will stay here," she responds.

Gavis debates taking her with him but decides against it. Just because he feels threatened by the human boy doesn't mean that Sara should be uprooted for it. He trusts her enough to be fine on her own. And he trusts the boy to be scared for his life for a few years.

As Gavis evaporates from the living room, Sara fiddles with the shower. The water is only extremely hot, without any cold. She sticks her hand under the spray and watches as her skin burns. She turns the knobs absently, wondering what she can do to fix it.

Finally, she gets up and wanders to the telephone.

×××

"Sven's Repair, we lock your locks and untie your knots," Sven barks into the receiver. His New York accent sounds like cash to the boys in the back.

Mason is one of those boys, taking a huge bite out of a sandwich. He's a lot younger than the other men and stands out wearing khaki shorts, a red t-shirt and his staple Converses. He chews slowly and sets the sandwich on the table at the sound of Sven's voice.

Customers have been slow for the past couple of days, and he's getting nervous. His family needs the money. The other men are getting anxious, too. They all look shiftily at each other. Usually they're friends, but when business is slow, it's every man for himself.

"We got a hot one!" Sven appears in the doorway, grinning.

Mason stands up so fast his chair topples backwards. He isn't alone, either. Men all over the room get to their feet.

"I've got this," Mason exclaims. He's clearly frustrated.

"Mason, calm the hell down," someone snaps at him.

"You ain't the only one with a family," another snarls.

"Mason's got this one, boys. He's worked the site before." Sven gestures for them to sit.

They do so, albeit reluctantly. Mason ignores the spiteful glances and mutterings. He concentrates on the fact that his family could really use the money.

"You gotta go back to the doll's place," Sven says to Mason.

"Which doll?" Mason asks. He's used to Sven's slang for women.

"The living doll. The one holed up with the magic man," Sven clarifies.

"Was it a man who called?" Mason is instantly wary.

"No, it was the doll, I tell you. Now get moving before I give the job to someone else."

Mason hesitates before picking up his toolbox and slipping out the back door. After a quick glance around, he sees his bike. It's incredibly old and rusted, and it's missing the seat, but it works and it was free. He sidesteps a woman taking a drag of her cigarette.

He's nervous because he doesn't know if Gavis has something to do with this. He's anxious to see Sara, but worried about what he'll say.

"Hey, Sara, sorry I blew you off," Mason mutters to himself. "You see, the thing is, I only didn't kiss you because I wanted to so much. You have no idea how much."

He slams his box onto the back of his bike. Grumbling incoherently, he secures it to the small metal shelf with a bungee cord. He plants one hand on the handlebars and the other on the fastened toolbox, and he kicks the stand.

It lets out a metallic groan and refuses to move. He kicks it again. And again. He comes away with the same results each time.

Mason takes a step back. He turns away from the bike and puts his hands to his head, looking up at the sky. He's still for a few tense seconds. Abruptly, he turns back and smashes his foot into the bike. It jumps away from him and clatters to the ground.

"And then there's Gavis and his damn fedora!" he shouts.

He stands for a moment before leaning down to jerk the bike back to a standing position.

"Got a problem with hats, buddy?"

He twists around to see the woman still smoking her cigarette. She looks at him, her expression bored. He watches her take her final drag before she crushes it out on the side of the building.

Mason deflates. "Sorry."

"Hey, man. Whatever floats your boat." She shrugs before turning and slouching into the building. Mason sees her shake her head before she's out of sight.

He turns back, bending down and wrenching up the kickstand with his hand. He wipes the rust on his shorts and steps on a bike pedal, balancing on the other as he pushes off.

It's a warm spring day with the breeze brushing the trees lining the street, making them sway. It also starts to dry the sweat sticking to Mason's brow as he peddles harder to get up a hill. He takes a shortcut through the park and notices a young couple sitting on a bench together, laughing. The girl waves at him as he passes.

He smiles, knowing they've cut school to be here together.

He dodges the few people on the sidewalk before turning on to Sara's road. It's void of all people but a girl in a pink dress standing outside of an apartment. Mason coasts to a stop a few feet away from her.

She doesn't look up, staring instead at the pavement beneath her feet. Her bangs are pulled back and clipped with a butterfly beret. The rest hangs breezily around her face. Her dress is shorter and pinker, though it is still clearly the same one from a few days ago. Gavis has changed it for her.

She doesn't acknowledge Mason's presence even as he struggles with the kickstand and finally gives up, leaning the bike on the side of the building. She rubs her injured hand against her dress as it begins to throb faintly.

"Hey," he gasps.

He comes to stand beside her, still breathing roughly from his ride. She doesn't look at him, but carefully considers the sidewalk. He notices smudges of color over her arms and legs, the pink stick of chalk dangling loosely in her fist. Other pieces of different colors are scattered around on the cracked sidewalk, pushed out of the way of a child-like drawing.

"Gavis likes it when I draw. He says it makes him remember his past." Sara squints at the cartoonish pink cat she's drawn.

"How so?" Mason asks. He's looking at her, not the cat.

"I never asked." Sara shrugs before meeting his gaze.

Looking into her remarkably blue eyes, Mason has a very strong urge to pull her into his arms, bury his face in her hair and never let go. Unnerved, he tries to shake it off but can't.

"The faucet is broken. There isn't any cold water," Sara explains. "Gavis isn't very good at household chores. Besides, he's gone."

"Gone?" Mason's brow furrows.

"Yes,"

"Where is he?"

"I don't know. He said he'd be back in a few days."

"A few days?" Mason asks incredulously.

"Yes. Gavis will return in a few days." Sara turns away, to the apartment.

Mason stands there for a second before grabbing his toolbox and following her quickly into the building. He doesn't notice a stick-figure drawing of a girl in a pink dress with yellow hair holding hands with a stick boy with brown hair and Converse high-tops.

Sara begins the ascent to her rooms, but Mason pauses at the base of the decrepit stairs, looking at all the doors hanging open in this portion of the building.

"Hey, Sara, what happened to all your neighbors?" Mason calls.

"They left." Sara doesn't glance down at him.

Mason begins to follow her up, almost tripping in his haste. He has a strange feeling she's angry with him, but he doesn't know what he did. Other than not come to see her, but he was here now, wasn't he? Besides, she wouldn't be able to be angry with him... would she?

He saunters through her front door, kicking it closed gently with his foot. He drops his toolbox, following her into the bathroom.

103

"Hey, are you mad at me or something?" he asks.

Sara sits on the floor, turning the knobs vaguely. "I can't feel anger, Mason. See how it's just hot water? It's only like that in the bathroom, though."

Mason can't understand why she won't look at him. "Yeah, I see it. Look, Sara, did I do something…?"

"No, nothing at all."

Mason doesn't understand that Sara has a one track mind. At the moment, she's focused on the faucet. Her behavior has absolutely nothing to do with him.

But Mason rubs the back of his neck, confused. He looks down at her fingers pressed against the side of the tub and stares.

"Jesus, what happened to your hand?"

Sara looks at it before turning to him. "That's how I found out there is only hot water. I burnt myself."

"Sara, you should have that looked at," Mason says, concerned.

"You've looked at it, haven't you?"

"No, I mean—"

"If you bring your tools in here, you can see what's wrong with the faucet."

104

Mason stares at her, even more incredulous, before backing out of the room. He shakes his head as he gets the box, remembering that she doesn't feel pain. He suddenly feels very angry at Gavis for having done this to her.

Meanwhile, Sara sticks her hand back under the scalding water. She watches as it pours down the sides, burning the flesh of her palm but not the back of her hand, where her string connects to her hand. She removes her fingers, flexing them, and stares down at the broken skin. She waits for a few seconds before replacing her hand under the spray, testing to see if it's gotten any cooler.

Just as the tips of her fingers breech the water, Mason appears in the doorway. His eyes go to her hand and he automatically shouts, "Sara, no!"

Terrible pain rips through Sara's hand and up her arm.

Mason drops his toolbox. He pulls her to her feet, dragging her through the bathroom and out into the kitchen. His thoughts are racing, but he knows what to do. There are countless injuries in his line of work.

Sara feels the pain this time. It's a searing hurt that shivers from her fingers to her shoulder and back down again. She thinks about the pain as she watches Mason slam on the tap and wrench open drawers.

"What are you looking for?" Sara asks.

"A washcloth or something. Don't you guys have anything to wash dishes with?" Mason exclaims. His frustrated tone causes Sara to cock her head to the side.

"We don't have any dishes. We don't eat."

Mason stares at her. Her mouth scrunches over to the side for a second, as she wonders why he doesn't answer her.

"No dishes," she repeats. "Ergo, nothing to wash them with."

Mason tosses a glance at the ceiling before yanking his shirt over his head. As he puts a corner in his mouth and pulls, ripping the fabric in smaller pieces, Sara looks at the ceiling. She wonders briefly what he'd been looking at.

Sara turns her attention back to him as he holds the shredded cloth under the running tap water, soaking it before turning back to her.

106

"Let me see your hand," he demands.

She obeys, holding her hurt fingers out to him. He wraps her hand with the cool cloth. She whimpers, evoking a flinch from him.

"Sorry, I'm sorry." He wraps his hands around her uninjured one. Sara glances down at their intertwined fingers before looking into his serious, dark eyes. "I've got to get you to the hospital, so no arguing, okay?"

"You're not wearing a shirt," Sara objects.

"C'mon."

Mason drags her to the door, slamming it closed behind her. She follows him absently, obeying his pleas for her to hurry up. She keeps bumping her hand on things, crying out without meaning to.

"Hold it close to you, okay? Like this." Mason grasps her wrist tenderly and presses the wet cloth to her dress.

He coaxes her outside, where she hesitates. "I told Gavis I'd stay here. I can't go to the hospital."

"I said no arguing, remember?"

"You did say that," Sara replies. "But I never agreed to it."

Mason ignores her, turning to… his bike. His one-person bike with no seat. Sara watches him stare at it. His ears turn a bit red. His expression becomes more agitated.

"Shit," Mason curses. He shoves a hand through his hair.

He steps out onto the street taking a quick look around. He seems to be looking for something specific, but Sara can't figure out what. She turns to look as well.

The roadway is completely blank, with only a few cars dotting the curb. Even though the day is warm, there are no children outside. Not one person climbs in or out of a car. Upon closer inspection, the other vehicles look abandoned.

"Where the hell are all the people?" Mason demands to no one in particular. His hands come to settle on his hips.

"They left," Sara replies.

Mason turns back to Sara. She's holding her hand just like he showed her, and she's watching him, with her head cocked a little. A slight breeze picks up and brushes some hair into her face. She blinks at him.

An idea dawns on him. "Do you have a cell phone?"

"What's a cell phone?" Sara asks.

"Shit." Mason crosses the street. "Shit, shit, *shit*."

She doesn't understand his actions, but something tugs in the pit of her stomach as she watches him pace around like a caged animal. It makes her want to throw her arms around him and pull him close, like in those black and white romantic movies she watches. She doesn't know what that means, but she wants to sit on the futon and think about it. She turns and reaches for the door handle.

"I'm going back inside," Sara announces.

"No! Wait." Mason jogs up to her, his arm outstretched. "I've got to get you to the—"

Sara whirls around and throws her arms around Mason's neck. Mason's arms encircle her waist and he stops.

"I knew you'd see me again. Gavis said you wouldn't, but I didn't believe him. I knew you'd come back," she whispers.

Mason moves his arms down, to avoid pushing her handle into her back. "Um, yeah, well—"

"Sara? Good Lord, is that you?"

Sara pulls away from Mason at the ring of a familiar voice. A woman stands a few feet from them, her hair covered by a wide-brimmed hat. She's wearing designer sunglasses, an expensive sundress and strappy high heels. She clutches a purse between her perfectly manicured hands, peering out at the two.

"Hello, Zalia," Sara calls.

"Actually, I go by Abana these days. You can call me Abby, though." The woman seems uncertain.

Mason is relieved. "I need to get to a hospital."

"Oh? What seems to be the trouble?" The woman frowns prettily.

"She's burnt her hand—"

The woman removes her darkened shades and Mason stops speaking. Her eyes are a violent shade of purple. Mason stands in front of Sara, glaring at the woman.

"I can actually feel it this time, Abby." Sara leans around Mason. "I'm in terrible pain."

"*Really*?" The woman blinks in surprise. "How interesting, Sara. What does Gavis have to say about that?"

"He's not here now," Sara explains. "But you must know that. You don't come and see me when Gavis is around."

"Well, this has been nice, but I've really got to take her to a doctor," Mason interrupts rudely.

"Abby's powerful. She can heal me." Sara grasps Mason's forearm.

"I don't feel comfortable with that, actually. We'll just be going now." He takes Sara's good hand and pulls her into the street, keeping his body between the woman and Sara.

"I'll come with you." The woman smiles.

Suddenly, the ground beneath Mason seems to drop out, and he feels the terrifying sensation of falling. Everything around him becomes a blur of colors, nothing really intelligible. And then it stops. The ground resurfaces, everything solidifies.

Mason is dazed, feeling off-balance. He's confused and extremely dizzy. Sara reaches out and takes his hand.

"Are you okay, Mason? You don't look well."

"Yeah, I'm fine." He shakes his head, trying to clear his vision.

"He's never jumped before, Sara. Give him some time." Abby reaches out towards Mason.

He waves his arm, dodging her grasp before losing his balance. He hits the sidewalk unsteadily.

"Do you need some help?" A nurse calls out from her cigarette break. She looks at them indecisively.

"No, thank you." Abby smiles at her.

The woman shrugs before taking a drag and turning away. Mason watches her before turning his eyes to Sara. She sits down on the ground next to him.

"Abby jumped us to the hospital." She smiles, putting a hand on his knee.

"I can see that." Mason looks down at his chest, seeing his soft red shirt instead of bare skin. "Um…?"

"I couldn't very well bring you here half naked," Abby replies. "Come along. Sara needs her hand looked at and you're sitting on the pavement like an idiot. The effects of jumping aren't that severe. You're being childish."

Abby breezes into the building, aware of Mason wrenching himself off the ground. Unsteadily, he helps Sara to her feet.

"This girl's hand has been burned severely," Abby announces once they're inside.

Several nurses scurry over, fluttering around Sara. They look curiously at her strings, and then glance at Abby. One look into the woman's purple eyes and they understand. They usher Sara into a separate hallway, away from her companions. She glances back at Mason before she rounds a corner and is gone.

Mason looks around the waiting room. It's a drab tan color that's supposed to make people feel calmer while they're waiting for news of their injured loved ones. Informative posters about abortion or smoking or what to do if someone's choking decorate the walls. Blue plastic chairs sit in orderly lines throughout the room like in an airport terminal. At the far end of the room, two secretaries sit behind a massive information desk. Four nurses lean against the counter and gossip quietly.

Mason's eyes rest briefly on a nervous couple sitting opposite him. They don't appear to be much older than he is, and the girl smoothes her hands over her stomach periodically. Mason looks away.

Abby looks directly at Mason. "Do you want to tell me how you did it?"

"Did what?" He moves away from her, slumping into a chair.

"How you gave Sara those emotions," Abby clarifies.

"I don't know what you're talking about," Mason says. "Please leave me alone."

"I've never seen anyone who could override Gavis' effect on people, especially when they aren't trying." Abby sits daintily in the chair next to him.

"I'm honestly not doing anything to try and work against Gavis. I was just doing a job and got tangled up in this whole thing," Mason snaps.

114

Abby stays silent for a moment, and Mason takes the time to look at the carpet. It's a woven blue and white pattern and annoyingly clean. He shudders to think of all the blood that must have stained it.

"Why are you so angry with me?" Abby asks.

"I don't know you. You obviously have magic. I can't trust you, can I? How do I know you aren't Gavis' spy or something?"

"Gavis' *spy*?" Abby laughs loudly. "Trust me, dear boy; Gavis doesn't need anyone's help to spy. And if he did, I would certainly *not* be the one."

Abby can tell he's interested by the sudden spark in his eyes. He says nothing for a while, looking over the waiting room critically.

"Yeah, whatever," he finally grumbles.

Abby is disappointed by his lack of trust. She decides to push on, anyway. "Whether you know it or not, you are counteracting Gavis' magic. Haven't you noticed how erratic Sara is? Take just now for instance. She was in such pain yet she threw her arms around you."

"Yeah, it was weird. But Sara's not like anyone else, you know? You just never know what to expect," Mason replies.

"Correction: *you* never know what to expect. I've known Sara since she was first turned, and she could never feel anything. Suddenly, you show up and she's feeling shadows."

"Shadows?" Mason's brow wrinkles.

"Ghosts of emotion, whispers of feeling. She burned her hand and she *felt* it, enough that she agreed to go to the hospital. And it's because of you." Abby's eyes sparkle.

She looks at the boy next to her, slumped down in the plastic blue chair. His expression is guarded, but he appears to be considering her words. She stares at him and thinks of Sara's behavior. She finally puts two and two together and understands. She's looking at the girl's soul-mate.

"But why me? What did I do?" Mason demands.

"You honestly don't know, do you?" Abby smiles wryly.

"Know *what*?"

116

"How do you feel about Sara?"

Mason finally looks at Abby, his dark eyes locking with hers. He stares at her for a few seconds before he glances away, leaning forward and putting his elbows on his knees. He studies the impeccably clean carpet, folds his hands and rests his chin on them.

"Well?" Abby encourages. She wants him to say it out loud.

Abby sees his will break. "I think I might"

"Mason!"

Mason's gaze snaps up to where Sara's standing. He shoots to his feet as a female doctor follows Sara over to him.

"Hey," Mason says before Sara throws her arms around him.

"Her hand was burned quite badly, but it started healing as soon as we took her to the back room. I honestly can't tell you when it will be fully healed, since I'm not gifted with magic, but at this rate of regeneration, I'd estimate just a few hours time," the doctor explains methodically. "If it doesn't heal or if there are any problems, don't hesitate to call us."

"Thank you," Mason says.

"I'm going to need someone to sign the release form. Are you her boyfriend?"

"Oh, no. No, we're not…" Mason looks down at Sara. She is still clinging to him; a brilliant smile spreads over her face. Abby watches him deliberate for a second. "Um, yeah. I am."

"Great. Just sign her out at the front desk." The doctor makes a benign gesture to the front of the room and walks away without a backwards glance.

Sara, meanwhile, wants to be as close to Mason as she can. When she went back into the doctor's office, she felt indifferent to the pain in her hand. Every minute she was back there, with all the nurses bustling around, her emotions seemed slip further away. When she caught sight of Mason, her hand had started to throb faintly. She realizes that he's the reason she's beginning to feel anything, and she doesn't want to let go. Besides, she wants to like the way he looks at her.

Mason tries to untangle himself from Sara, needing to head over to the front desk. Sara clings to him, but Abby manages to peel her off. The two watch Mason stride over to the front desk and take the clipboard from the nurse. He smiles slightly before slouching against the counter. He starts to take a look at the forms.

"Haven't you noticed she's intent on touching you?" Abby says, materializing beside him.

Mason is startled, and slams his elbow into the corner of the counter. He winces and rubs it roughly. He snaps at her, "Jesus, could you not do that? You almost gave me a heart attack."

"Did you notice?" Abby presses.

"Yeah, I guess," Mason hedges. He's obviously uncomfortable.

"She knows that her emotions start to surface when she's close to you." Her purple eyes try vainly to catch Mason's gaze.

"You can't possibly know that."

"I do, though. I also know that you—"

"Sir, I'm going to have to ask you to sign out and move on. You're holding up the line." A nurse taps the desk impatiently.

"Oh, sorry." Mason quickly scribbles his initials in the designated slots.

"Mason, have you been listening to anything I've been saying?" Abby hisses.

"No, not really. I'm having a...a... sensory overload right now."

"A sensory overload," Abby repeats slowly.

"Yeah. Sara burns her hand; you show up, you whisk us away through time and space..." Mason pauses to take a deep breath. "It's just a lot to take in."

"You're not used to magic," Abby realizes. She follows Mason away from the counter.

"No, definitely not," Mason snorts.

"Perhaps if I explained things to you," she muses.

"Can it wait?" Mason asks. "I've got to get Sara home first."

Abby sighs and lets Mason walk away from her. She knows there won't be any talking to him seriously until he's not focused on Sara any longer. They approach her and she smiles, reaching out for Mason.

As soon as her hand slips into his, he feels himself falling. Abby senses Mason's panic before Sara's living room appears all around them. He manages to stay

120

standing this time, and he waits impatiently for the vertigo to pass.

"What do you plan to do, Mason?" Abby asks.

He ignores her, stumbling into the bathroom and shutting off the still-running water. Abby watches, amused, as Sara ghosts after him, following him into, then out of, the small room.

Abby takes the time to look around the apartment. It's the first time she's ever been inside, and it's not at all what she expected. The place is almost bare, it's dusty, and it looks like the hiding place of a desperate man. She's gripped by a sudden, overwhelming sadness. *Gavis, what happened to you?*

Abby takes a step back as Mason practically sprints to the closet, grabbing Sara's broken doll. As he slams the door, he turns and reaches for Sara's hand, not bothering to avoid touching her string.

"What are you doing?" Sara asks.

"Gathering your things… er, thing," Mason explains. "You're coming to stay with me."

"But Gavis—"

"We'll leave a note," Mason says firmly. "Is there anything else you want to bring?"

Sara stands, her hand in his, hesitating. "Mason…"

"Do you trust me?" Mason asks.

Abby watches Sara search his face. "Yes."

Abby can see as well as sense Mason's surprise. He wasn't really expecting her to answer him so quickly.

"Completely?" he tests.

"Yes."

Abby can see the honesty in her clear, blue eyes. She feels a change in his emotions as distinct as night and day. Surprised, she is sucked into his head.

He's imagining it all in one, fluid movement; reaching up to cup her face, moving closer, looking down into her eyes, moving closer and closer until her lips – slightly parted – are only millimeters away…

Abby snaps back into her own mind with force. Sara and Mason stand away from each other, hand in hand, memorizing each other's faces.

"I assume you need paper and a pen to write your note," Abby interrupts.

Mason looks up, snapping back to reality. Abby concentrates on a little coffee shop downtown, one that she goes to often. She remembers seeing a pen on the counter, for customers to use. She focuses on the thought of it. The object appears in her hand, and she holds it out to Mason.

"Thanks." He keeps his eyes down.

Abby watches Mason take a seat on the fold out bed, his gaze on the paper. Sara is watching him, too, Abby notes. She reaches out to Sara telepathically, feeling her mind.

Surprisingly, Sara is also thinking of a possible kiss from Mason. She imagines it, feeling a slight flicker inside her.

Abby shakes her head, withdrawing back into herself. She understands their bond, though she can't feel it like Gavis does. These two, whether they know it or not, are destined to be together.

So she can't comprehend Mason's sudden hesitation. He was so ready to take her home a few minutes ago, but now he is staring at the paper, deep in thought.

"Mason?" Sara prompts quietly.

His head snaps up and he meets her gaze. Abby is very nearly sucked into his head again. She fights to stay inside her own mind, but Mason's thoughts come across loud and clear.

He has a family. A large one, desperate for money. If he takes Sara and Gavis gets really angry, he could bring hell down around them all. Is Sara worth that risk?

Abby balances on the tipping slide of Mason's emotions. As he snaps to a decision, she is once again cast from his mind.

No wonder he's never had much dealing with magic before, Abby thinks. *He's a bloody black hole. No one with real power could stand to be around him for long. He's giving me a migraine.*

"Can you jump us to my house?" Mason asks, scribbling on the paper.

"Sure. All you have to do is think about it. Visualize it," Abby replies absently. She's still deep in thought.

"Alright, let's go." Mason stands.

Abby watches with interest as he grabs Sara's hand and starts towards her. "Now?"

"Yeah, now. Before I change my mind."

Abby smiles and feels the shift as she jumps them through space. The picture in Mason's mind becomes clearer to her. She lets out a deep breath and the ground reappears beneath her feet.

After a brief pause, Sara asks, "So, this is where you live, Mason?"

Mason looks at the house, slightly ashamed. "Yeah, this is it."

"It's got character." Sara smiles at the building.

Mason merely snorts, taking the steps two at a time and shoving back the door. It's rusty hinges screech, but he doesn't seem to notice.

Abby follows Sara into the house, pushing Sara's handle inside with her foot before closing the door. Abby hears Mason swear under his breath.

"What's wrong?" Abby looks around curiously.

Mason seems embarrassed that she heard him. "Um, I left my toolbox at Gavis' place."

Abby remembers seeing it. She pulls it out of the apartment with her mind and hands it to Mason.

"Er, thanks." He takes it from her hesitantly.

"Mason's home!"

"He's back!"

"Mason!"

A herd of children tumble down the stairs, screaming and laughing. As soon as they see Abby and Sara, they stop, the smiles dying on their faces. Only one of his sisters pushes through her siblings and rushes to hug Mason.

"Oh, Mason! You're back so early!" she crows.

"Yeah, I had a little… incident at the apartment," Mason laughs, swinging her tiny frame around.

"Who are these people?" One older boy glares at Abby.

"Sara and Abby." Mason tries to set his sister down, but she clings to him.

"She's got purple eyes," another points out. "Ma's not going to be happy."

"Is this the Sara you've been telling us about?" the girl in his arms asks.

126

Mason's face turns pink. "Uh, yeah. Look, why don't you guys go upstairs, alright? Where's Ma?"

"In the kitchen." The kids begin to back away.

"Alright, then. Off you go." Mason sends the kids upstairs before turning back to the two women. "Sorry about the house, I haven't had the time to repaint or anything…"

"I think it's lovely," Sara says.

"Um, thanks."

Mason turns and heads into the kitchen. As Abby passes, she taps the wall gently. The wallpaper brightens and reattaches itself to the wall. She brushes her fingertips against the banister on the steps and a shiny new coat of paint bubbles to the surface. Abby heads into the kitchen.

"She's got nowhere else to go, Ma," Mason pleads.

"I'm sorry, Sara. I bet you're a very nice girl, but I have a lot of mouths to feed, and not a lot of money or space."

Abby watches Mason's mother cross her arms. The woman looks extremely tired and overwhelmed. She also seems to be confused. She's staring at Mason's fingers interlocked with Sara's.

"Ma, this isn't really up for negotiation. Either she's staying here or I'm going with her." Mason leans on the counter, looking steadily at his mother.

"Is that right? And where would you be staying?" Even though her words are forceful, the woman falters.

"You know Johnny down at the motel is hiring. I could get a full time job there and he'd give us a room. I could pay for food with my earnings and you wouldn't have to worry about feeding me anymore."

Abby can see the panic rise in Mason's mother and worries about her heart. She feels the need to help the poor woman. "What if Sara paid rent?"

"Don't be ridiculous. You know she doesn't have any money," Mason tells her.

"Right, but I do." Abby reaches into her purse and pulls out a roll of one-hundred dollar bills. "Is this enough for now?"

The kitchen falls silent. Abby watches Anita's lips purse, her eyes narrow. She considers the wad of cash for a bit while Abby holds it out steadily.

"That's plenty." Anita takes the money and puts it in her bra. Safest place for it in this neighborhood. Her eyes pan over the three, lingering on Sara's strings and Abby's eyes. "You better know what you're doing, Mason. I'm going upstairs to lie down. You missed dinner, but I kept it in the oven for you."

Abby watches her leave, thinking that she must have been a beautiful woman once. She just looks exhausted and too old now.

"Well, that's… quite a lot of money." Mason stares suspiciously at Abby. She rolls her eyes in response.

One of Mason's little sisters dashes into the kitchen. "Mason, I'm having a tea party!"

"Good for you, Marcy," Mason smiles.

"I want Sara to be my extinguished guest!" Marcy slips her hand into Sara's and smiles brightly.

"It's a *distinguished* guest, Marcy, and I don't really think—"

"I've never been to a tea party before," Sara interrupts.

Mason thinks it over. "Alright. Okay, go have fun."

"Thanks, Mason!" Marcy laughs before dragging Sara out of the room.

Abby smiles at Sara's retreating form before she looks over at Mason. "We need to talk, anyway."

"What about?" He looks back at her, his expression guarded.

Two cups of coffee materialize from a Starbucks downtown. Abby hands one to Mason and looks down into the other. "You might want to sit down. You see, I have a story to tell you…"

Part Four

You don't know Gavis, but I do. Very well, in fact.

Gavis and I are two of a kind. Not like humans and not much like the rest of the immortals. Immortals *can* be killed, if harmed by blunt force. We can live forever, only if we keep ourselves safe. I know this because I was born in Sparta, in what people now refer to as the year 431 BCE.

That's where Gavis and I met. We could sense each other's power, and after an initial phase of fear and mistrust, we fell in love. Don't give me that face, boy; Gavis was a *good* man back then. He was honest and loyal and charismatic. It was impossible not to love him.

We wed and shortly after, we stopped aging. Just like that. We had to move from Sparta and ever since then, we never lived in one place for more than a few years. But we had each other and that was enough.

Magic's a funny thing. It makes you more than human, but it short-wires some of your natural abilities. Both of us were sterile. Or so we assumed, since we were together for hundreds of years and I never bore children. It wasn't until 1822 that I got pregnant. We hailed it as a miracle. I was pregnant for an incredibly long time: about two years, in fact. I credited this to my extensive life. And we had a girl. A little blonde, insanely beautiful, girl.

I was happy, but not as much as Gavis. He'd always wanted to have children, and it pained him to pass through time without any.

Again, magic is a funny thing. I'm not going to try and fool you—I've never met anyone with as much power as I have. Gavis would be right behind me, if there were a scale. We are, to date, the most powerful people who have lived. So, something must have gone wrong when our powers mixed together. Our little girl couldn't handle the amount of magic she possessed.

When she was a toddler, she'd throw a tantrum and destroy a town. She'd cry and bust the windows out of every shop on the street. When she'd get angry, she could literally take your skin off. We kept her—and everyone else—safe by living in the mountains, away from civilization.

She grew to the age of nine and then stopped aging. Forever stuck as a child, she was unable to control at least one of her powers. As the years passed and more and more powers surfaced, they began to change her. The levels of magic in her had never before been seen. It, quite literally, drove her insane.

She didn't recognize us anymore. She went out of control. I feared for the world, because she had the magic within her to kill us all in the blink of an eye. Gavis and I did what we had to do to keep the humans safe. We had to... remove... our only child. Our baby girl.

Gavis was the one who did it. He wanted to spare me from the horror. He did, I guess. But it changed him. He couldn't stand the thought of what he had done. He became distant from me, and eventually, he left. Without saying goodbye, without an explanation. Just... gone. I was heartbroken.

It wasn't until the 1930's that I found him again. I then discovered the monster that he'd become.

He'd been tricking little, blonde, nine year old girls to agree to be his puppets.

Gavis had a theory; if he had taken away our little girl's emotions, she wouldn't have gone so out of

136

control. He could have saved her, if he had made her into a numb, unfeeling child.

He was stripping the girls of their emotions and putting them on display for money. It was his way of keeping our daughter close to him. He believed he was saving these children by giving them a better life then they would have had without him. He still believes this.

I have tried to change his mind, but he sees me as a threat. I've been tracking him, talking to the girls whenever he's away, trying to find a solution to his spell. You see, even though I'm more powerful than he is, our magic is too different for me merely to undo his misdeeds.

Truthfully, I've never been as close to any of the girls as I am to Sara. I have never been able to save any of his victims before, but I believe I've found the key. It's you.

There is a… well I guess you'd call it a rumor, that's whispered through the magical society. It's believed that every person has a soul mate.

It's said that the pull to your soul mate is undeniable, that you can't resist him or her. You can't help but fall in love. The problem is that there are billions of people on the planet and you only have one soul mate. You could live in America your whole life and your soul mate could be in the U.K. and you'd die without meeting each other. It's rare that anyone finds their soul mate. But it does sometimes happen.

I think you've found yours. I think, with my entire being, that it's Sara. That's why you are the only one who can save her.

When you're around her, she begins to feel shadows. You bring them out of her. When you leave, the shadows retreat, leaving her as blank as before.

Gavis' magic isn't very complicated. He doesn't remove emotions—he merely cloaks them from the heart. He can only manipulate people, not pull things from them. The only problem is that when one's heart goes without feeling for too long, one is no longer considered human. Nature rebels against this anomaly by changing the physical being. Gavis' puppets eventually turn into just that: stiff, unmoving, unfeeling puppets.

Sara's nearly to that place. She can't eat, drink, sleep. She's changing into what Gavis wanted her to be. But I believe that you can save her. You are her only chance.

Sometimes we people with magic come across someone whom we refer to as a 'black hole.' This person has a mind unlike that of most humans; it literally sucks us in and unbalances our powers. I don't wonder why you haven't had to deal with us before. You are a black hole. Being around you just gives us major headaches. But you have the power to use your mind as a weapon against us. You are a threat to Gavis—an even greater one than I am.

Part Five

Mason looks down at the coffee-to-go cup pressed in his palms, letting his skin leech the warmth from the cardboard. He's not much of a coffee drinker, mostly because they can't afford it, but he rather likes the flavor.

"Well?"

He looks up at Abby. She seems different to him, more defeated. She'd started her story cool and detached, but that had changed when she had spoken about her daughter. He can see that she's being honest but he doesn't know what to think anymore. Tears that filled her eyes when she had talked about the death of her daughter still clung there, making the purple seem brighter, making the woman look hundreds of years younger than she claimed to be.

"What do you want me to say?" he asks.

"Anything," Abby replies.

Mason turns his gaze back to his cup. He also doesn't know what to say.

"Why did Sara call you two different names?" he finally asks.

"What?"

"When she first saw you she called you a name, something weird. But you told her you go by Abby now. Why?"

Abby's expression clears. "Every couple of decades I change my name. I get bored with it so I choose a new one. I like to choose names with meaning. My pervious name was Zalia, which means power. Abby's short for Abana, which means everlasting."

"Because you live forever."

Mason sits back in his chair, letting the old wood dig into his back. It's keeping him grounded. The chair creaks slightly as it bears his weight. Mason knows he shouldn't even be sitting on it. It's old and could break at any time. He's been saving money for some new ones, but he had to forfeit the cash to pay bills.

"You're not even thinking about Sara." Abby pinches the bridge of her nose between her thumb and forefinger.

"Sorry, no. Can you, like, read my mind or something?" Mason asks.

"Occasionally. It's not that I have the ability to read minds, but as a black hole, you suck me in. I see the

144

world from your eyes for brief moments, until I can get a hold of myself."

Mason's lips press into a thin line. "I'm not sure how I feel about that."

"Well, it doesn't really matter since neither of us can control it," Abby snarks.

"You said I give you people headaches," he continues. "Do you have one now?"

"More like a migraine. But the caffeine helps." She smiles very slightly and shakes the liquid in the bottom of the cup.

"Does Gavis know what I am?" Mason asks. His fingers tighten on his cup.

Abby cocks her head. "I assume not. I doubt you'd be alive if he did. He never was good at finding people like you."

"Why?"

"It's his power. He lives inside other people so much he doesn't even realize the change in the mind. His full attention is usually on the emotions themselves," Abby explains.

"But what about the headaches?" Mason persists. "I mean, if I gave him a migraine, he'd notice, right?"

"Not necessarily." Abby shakes her head. "Overuse of powers can cause migraines. Exhaustion, transporting... it doesn't take a lot. You get used to them."

Mason looks around the kitchen, trying to absorb all this information while simultaneously trying *not* to think about what Abby has said he and Sara are...

"Do you believe in love-at-first-sight, Mason?" Abby asks softly.

"No, actually. I think to fall in love at first sight is shallow. I mean, you don't really know the person, do you? You just look at her outer appearance and decide right then."

"You think love is a decision?" Abby asks.

"I dunno. I mean, I guess. Like, my ma didn't have to stay with my father, but she did, even when he, you know, hit her. It's more of a choice, isn't it? Gavis chose to leave you and think of you as an enemy, when he could have stayed and healed with you and kept on loving you. But he didn't." Mason blows out a breath and looks at the floor.

"What about happy endings?"

"What about them?"

"Do you believe in them?"

Mason looks back at Abby, irritated. "Look, this isn't some book a teenage girl is writing, alright? This is real life. Real life doesn't have fairy-tale endings. Sad, broken shells of people try to do the best they can. Life is about money, social combat and sex. Life sucks and then you die. The. End."

Abby looks at the young man through sad eyes. He's turned his face from her, but she can see the pain etched in the stiffness of his shoulders, the rough way he shoves his hand through his hair. He's too cynical for his age, too exposed to the black and white film of time. Even his hands belong to an old man: calloused, stained and bruised.

"Is that what you think when you look at Sara?" she asks.

Mason's breath hitches as her words clang around the inside of his skull. He can't think; he's confused. The possibility is too damning, frightening, *impossible.*

"Well?" Abby persists.

Mason doesn't answer her. He rips the label off his cup slowly, concentrating fully on it.

Abby's her head is pounding. She's becoming increasingly frustrated by the seconds slipping by. A large part of her wants to just jump somewhere else, to get away from him. Her other, more sensible part realizes that he'll talk. She just needs to push him a bit more.

"Fine. I can tell when I'm looking at a lost cause."

Mason's dark eyes meet hers, shocked. She twists her mouth into a bitter smile.

"You don't want to help her. You've got a family here to take care of, and I get that. Don't worry; soon she'll be a puppet anyway, so you don't have to explain to her that you won't be seeing her anymore." Abby sets her cup on the edge of the bar as she turns to leave. "I suggest taking her home before Gavis comes back. As you know, he's got a nasty temper."

Mason watches the woman walk into the hall, hears the door open and rattle shut behind her before he can get his brain to work. He slams his coffee cup on the counter and dashes to the door, wrenching it open. Abby's in the middle of the street by now. If she hears him, she shows no sign of it. She doesn't stop.

"Wait!" Mason shouts.

Abby turns to see him stumbling down the stairs. She doesn't know what he wants, but she's about done listening to his internal struggle. Unless he's going to say something that will give her a clue he might be interested in saving Sara, she's made up her mind she's not going to listen.

Mason lurches to a stop. "No."

"No what?" Abby asks.

"The answer to your question is no. Sara doesn't make me think that way. She opens new doors and lets me relax, lets me be myself without having to think of all the work I have to do at home, or worry about the money in the bank, or dread tomorrow.

"But that's crazy, isn't it? I mean, I've only seen her, what, three times? Sane people don't just fall in

149

love with someone after being with that person three times!"

Abby takes Mason in. His face is suddenly flushed and agonized, his expression passionate. She watches his chest rise and fall with his accelerated breathing, his hands balled into fists at his side.

"It's crazy, right?" he repeats.

A tiny smile touches her lips. "True love is never sane."

Mason stands for a second, and his expression reminds Abby of a confused puppy. He shakes his head minutely. She doesn't know what he had expected her to say, but it obviously wasn't this. She's thrown him into turmoil.

"Mason?" a voice calls.

Mason jerks around to see Sara standing in the doorway, her hands cupping her elbows. The light from the hallway illuminates her hair, making her look like an angel with a halo. Seeing her, he's even more confused than he was before.

He turns back to Abby. She's gone. Twilight has descended upon the avenue, and the city mandated

street lamps are flickering on. A rogue newspaper
rustles its way into a gutter, carried by the slight breeze.

"Mason?"

He doesn't turn. "Yeah?"

"Your mother put your siblings to bed. She wanted
me to come find you," Sara explains.

"Um, yeah. Abby just…" He gestures to the empty
space around him.

"Teleported, I know. She does that." Sara smiles at
him, though he doesn't see.

Mason stares where Abby used to be, unnerved not
only by her sudden disappearance, but by their
conversation. It was definitely not what he wanted to
hear. But, then again, when did good news ever come
his way?

"Your mother said it was okay for me to spend the
night," Sara continues.

Well, Mason supposes, *this is* extremely *good news*.
He'll take back his previous thought.

"I'll clean up my room a bit for you," he replies. He
turns and starts towards Sara, not quite meeting her
eyes.

151

"Your mom already prepared the couch for me."
She watches him climb the stairs slowly, stopping on
the second to the top.

"Sara, you can't sleep on the couch," Mason scoffs.

"Why not?" Her head tilts slightly to the side.

"Because you're a guest," Mason says. *Because it's
a piece of junk and we can't afford a new one,* he
thinks.

"Oh. I thought you were alluding to the fact that I
can't sleep." Sara smiles sweetly, her fingers twisting
around her strings coyly.

Mason hesitates. "Are you proving some kind of
point?"

"Yes!" she laughs. "I don't need to sleep, Mason.
So, it's only fair that you should sleep in your own
room."

Her smile makes his heart twist. He can't argue with
her any longer. "Okay, I surrender."

Sara laughs some more as he holds up his hands and
gives her an impish smile. But she can see his eyes are
troubled. She's not sure what happened while she was
playing with Marcy, but she assumes it wasn't good.

"You should go to sleep," she sighs.

His brow creases. "What makes you say that?"

Sara reaches out and touches his face lightly with her fingertips. "Your eyes. They have shadows around them."

Mason closes his eyes, leaning into her palm slightly. He thought being around Sara would calm him, but it seems to be making him as confused as ever.

"Mason?" Sara whispers tentatively.

"Mhmm?"

"Is something wrong?"

Mason tenses, and his eyes flash open. "What do you mean?"

"I don't know." Sara shakes her head slowly. "You seem a little... upset."

Mason draws away from Sara's touch. "No, nothing's wrong. Everything's cool."

"Cool?"

Sara keeps her gaze on Mason's her blue eyes clear and untroubled. She wants to worry about him, but can't. She tries to let it go, but can't do that either. It seems to be harder, these days, to give up on things.

"You're probably right. I should get to bed," Mason says.

Sara nods but does not understand the subtle change that has just occurred in Mason. One second he's open and letting her get close to him, and the next, he's distant, his expression drawn. She stares at him for a few seconds, wrapping her strings around her hands, to pick the handle off the floor.

Sara steps lightly back away from the door, never dropping her gaze from his. He lifts one eyebrow, walking towards her, also keeping their eyes locked. This little game persists until Mason reaches the base of the steps. Sara turns to leave, to go into the living room.

"Sara?"

She about-faces. Mason's on the second stair, paused in his ascent. He breaks out in a broad smile.

"Goodnight."

Sara smiles back, a reflex of that once-upon-a-time when she had emotions. "Goodnight, Mason."

×××

Midnight.

154

She knows this, because the old, ticking clock on the wall says so. It has strange symbols where the numbers should be, but she remembers through the fuzzy filter of memories that her mother had a clock like this one. An antique time keep with Roman Numerals.

Sara's eyes track a moth as it flits off the top of the clock on dust powdered wings and starts a swirling, twirling dance through the air. Her bright eyes, shining like large, iridescent orbs in the near darkness, follow the lone insect as it struggles to the window on the other side of the room. Pale light spills in, cutting four perfect rectangles onto the floor.

She's been sitting for hours, in this exact spot, moving only her head and fingers, as she has twisted and untwisted the material of her dress. Her hair has been fixed in her ponytail, every strand kept back and neat.

Sara looks back at the clock, her head tilting to the side to see it up so high. Just an hour before, Abby had arrived.

Sara had been sitting in this exact position, doing just as she was now. Abby teleported into the light beams by the window, and in the spotlight, Sara could see wisps of purple magic clinging to the woman, moving like protective, misty tendrils around her as she solidified. She shook them off before moving to Sara.

Sara said nothing, moved only her head to look up at Abby. Abby bent down and whispered just two lines into Sara's ear. Then, she kissed Sara's temple and began to walk away. Just as the light hit her again, she vanished in a violet, dusty cloud.

Sara thinks about what Abby had told her. Something within Sara stirs, like a creature reemerging after a long winter. She swallows and moves her head in a circle, trying to either force the feeling away or strengthen it, she doesn't know.

Trust in Mason. He will save you.

Sara feels the stirring again, only much more violently. There is something in the words, some kind of magic that creates this inside her. Sara is sure it must be pain, but she can't think clearly anymore. Her brain seems to be heavy.

156

Sara lets her head tilt back, closing her eyes and letting her lips fall open. She listens to her steady breathing as it deepens and slows.

Trust in Mason. He will save you.

Mason.

Sara gets off the couch, stepping around it. She paces through the kitchen, up the stairs.

The only sound in the house is her feet padding on the old, wooden floor, as she walks down the hall, past doors slightly ajar, with children sleeping in the bellies of the rooms. Sara doesn't pause to look at the dim overhead light on the ceiling She does notice, however, two flies bumping against it with delicate *thunk*s.

At the end of the hallway is a door, crooked on its hinges, firmly shut. Sara hesitates at the old wood, pressing her fingertips to the slightly rusted knob. This is the room Marcy gestured to, openly jealous that the person who lives here is the only one in the whole house with a room of his own, aside from her mother.

Sara braces her left palm on the door while the right twists the knob and slides it open.

A sliver of light from the hall appears on a pair of feet, sweeps up faded jeans and onto a naked stomach as the door opens wider.

Mason's one arm is thrown across his face, the other onto the pillows pulled down beside him. A heavy blanket is tossed to the floor, a thin sheet tangled in his legs, proof of his restless night. His t-shirt lies in a crumpled ball on the floor, his shoes and socks haphazardly tossed in a corner, where he threw them before he crashed. Next to the clothes are stacks of books, with old, worn covers.

Sara slips in and closes the door gently, resting against it. The bulb from the hall isn't the only source of light in the room; a high placed window casts four rectangles on Mason's face and chest, which, Sara concludes, is the reason his arm covers his eyes. Sara crosses to the bed, skirting it, moving to the more vacant side of the mattress.

As she sits down and takes off her shoes, Mason stirs at the shift in the bed.

"Ugh?"

Sara draws her legs up, taking her hair out of its ribbon before lying down and curling into the pillow tucked into Mason's side, placing her head in the crease of his elbow.

"Sara?" Mason's open eyes look at her blearily.

"Hello, Mason," she whispers.

"Wha… what're you doin' here?"

"Something happened."

"What?"

Mason sits up, but Sara's head is lying on part of his arm. He repositions himself on the elbow she's resting on. He wipes a line of drool from the corner of his mouth with the back of his hand, slightly embarrassed and significantly more awake.

Sara's eyes feel incredibly heavy. She closes them, relaxing further into Mason's arm.

"What happened, Sara?" Mason asks. He'd meant to say it forcefully, but it came out softer, tenderly.

He sees her lips move gently, like she's whispering a secret too low for him to hear. And then she's out.

Mason rubs his chin, looking down at her. He blows a breath out through his nose, one side of his mouth quirking up slightly as he glances around. He struggles to free himself of the covers and then pulls the pillow out from between Sara and himself.

She murmurs something unintelligible, wriggling closer to him, sliding her head in the dip of his shoulder like two jigsaw pieces slipping together. He waits until she's settled before tucking the sheet around her, mindful of her strings.

He lies back against his pillows, a smile twisting its way onto his lips. He closes his eyes and rolls his head in her direction, into her blonde hair, breathing deep. He loves the way she smells.

Opening his eyes, he brushes the loose curls off her face, tucking them behind her ear. She doesn't move, her lashes creating little shadows on her cheeks in the moonlight.

Mason knows he won't be able to fall asleep, not now that she's here. He's never slept very well, not since his father died and he's had everything to worry about. It's a miracle he ever sleeps at all.

He rolls his head back to look at the ceiling and closes his eyes.

Yet, just a few minutes later, he, too, falls into a deep, dreamless sleep.

×××

Sara comes to her senses slowly, aware of one thing at a time.

She's pressed against something warm. She opens her eyes and sees only skin. She remembers where she was last night, concluding this must be Mason. She twists her head, trying to see better.

She and Mason are tangled together. One of his arms is under her head, the other around her waist. Their legs are twisted in the sheets. His face is buried in her hair, and she can feel his warm breath there, feel his chest move in and out slowly.

Sara blinks. She can *feel* him. She lets her forehead rest back against his chest, where it was when she opened her eyes.

And she slept, didn't she? That's what the disorientation was about, the heavy feeling in her brain. She's still a little fuzzy, but steadily gaining perception.

But, God, she can *feel.* She tries to feel surprised. Nothing comes to the surface, but she can feel it hover just below, waiting.

Trust in Mason. He will save you.

She presses herself closer to him. Blindly, she reaches up and traces his bare arms. He's toned and Sara remembers how hard he has to work, how physical his job is.

Her hand runs back up his arm, crossing down onto his chest. She takes a deep breath and feels his abs tense as she presses her fingertips to them.

But, God, I can feel.

Mason draws back slightly, his eyes blinking open. Sara turns her face to his, her expression serious.

"Did I wake you?" she asks quietly.

Mason smiles, closing his eyes. He bends down and presses his face into her neck, pulling her closer. He breathes deep, pauses, then chuckles.

"Yeah, you did. But, honestly, I don't mind."

Sara's breath catches in her throat. She strains up against him, letting his arms flex around her. *Feeling is so good.*

162

After an agonizingly brief moment, he pulls away from her, flopping back onto the bed. She watches one side of his mouth quirk up into a dry smile. He doesn't meet her eyes, but instead looks to the ceiling.

"I haven't slept that well in... well, in years, I guess." He yawns.

Sara wiggles closer to him, sitting up and propping herself on one hand. She places her other hand cautiously on his chest, searching for his dark gaze.

"Mason?"

His familiar eyes meet hers, but now they're worried. She looks down at him as he waits for her to go on, and she wonders briefly how she looks to him. She wonders what it would be like to look through his eyes. She shakes herself.

"Something changed," she continues.

"What?"

"I slept last night, for the first time. And, I can... I... *feel*."

Mason sits up, his hand covering hers on his chest. "Really?"

She cocks her head. "Not emotions, but touch."

"You're crying." Mason reaches out and rubs his thumb against some tears in the corner of her eye. "It's-it's like I'm experiencing the emotions but not feeling them fully. Almost but not quite." She shakes her head. "I don't know how to explain it."

Mason leans back and shoves his hand through his hair. He twists off the bed, away from Sara's touch. She keeps her hand raised for a second before letting it drop.

She watches as Mason paces. She wipes the stray tears off her face, marveling at the drops on her fingers. She presses them into the bed, watching the dents her fingers make in the mattress disappear when she lifts her hand.

Mason stumbles to the dresser in the corner and rummages through a drawer. He pulls out another pair of jeans, a shirt and some boxers. He balls them in between his hands, his brow creased, his jaw clenched. He turns and crosses back to the bed.

Sara reaches out for him, on her knees by this point. He drops the shirt on the floor and takes her face gently

164

in his hands. Sara encircles his wrists with her long, pale fingers.

"Don't be upset, okay? I can't stand it. I'll save you. I don't know how, not yet, but it'll happen, alright?" he promises, fiercely.

Sara just nods, feeling the twisting happening inside her again. She wonders if he's going to kiss her now. Her breathing hitches.

"Mason, mom wanted me to tell you—" Josephine throws open Mason's door, clothes basket in hand.

She stops speaking as Mason steps away from Sara, his expression dark. She watches one of his hands settle on his hip and the other rub the back of his neck. He stares at his sister for a short second.

"What, Josie?" he growls.

The younger girl is obviously flustered and embarrassed. Her eyes dart from her brother to Sara, and then back to Mason. "Um, you don't have to go to work today. Apparently we came into some money last night and besides—" she looks pointedly at Sara. "— you have a guest."

"Okay. Thanks." Sara watches as he crosses his arms, looking at the floor.

"I'll be back for your clothes later." Josephine glances at Sara again. "The, um, the bathroom's open." With that she leaves, kicking the door open further. This only seems to aggravate Mason. He blows out a breath, his shoulders slumping. He shakes his head at the retreating figure of his sister. Sara twists her fingers in her dress, absorbed in everything he does.

Finally he sighs, turning and wrapping Sara in his arms. Her hands come up around his neck, and she closes her eyes. She feels him relax and wonders if this offers him any source of comfort, this small touch. She thinks about how drastically he's changed her already and holds him tighter, wanting to give him whatever he needs. After a few seconds, he untangles himself from her, reaching down and scooping up his clothes.

"I'm gonna take a shower. Everyone's probably downstairs, so you can go meet them if you want," he says without looking at her.

She watches him walk away, wrapping her arms around herself. She feels the absence of him and wonders if he feels the same.

×××

About two seconds into the shower, the hot water stops working.

Mason resists the urge to cry out. Instead, he tries to rinse his hair out as quickly as possible.

At least the frigid water takes care of his, uh hem, little problem. He found, as he cleared the tub of Barbie dolls and toy boats, that the more he thinks of Sara, the more his blood heats.

But it isn't like the change in water temperature takes him by surprise. He lets everyone take their baths before him, so they use all the hot and leave him with the cold. *It's good for endurance,* he almost convinces himself as he tries to be speedy and thorough with the soap. *You know, in case I ever swim the English Channel or climb Mount Everest.*

He rolls his eyes—shivering, lips blue—as he shuts off the water. He wraps a towel around his waist and steps from the shower, to the sink.

He sorts through the mess until he comes across a blue toothbrush labeled *mason*. He squeezes some toothpaste onto it and sticks it in his mouth, wiping the little steam from the cracked mirror with his forearm.

The door swings open and a dark-haired girl steps through. Mason chokes on his toothbrush, coughing as his sister closes the door.

"Josie, what the hell? I'm *naked*—"

"Oh, like I haven't seen it before," she snorts.

Mason spits into the sink, glaring at her.

"We can't have another mouth to feed, Mason," Josephine says steadily.

"What? She's paying for room and board, so I don't really think—"

The door opens wider and two other girls slip in. Mason groans in frustration. "I don't think you guys understand the severity of this situation. You see, under this towel, I happen to be stark naked—"

"Like we haven't seen it before," Lisa grunts.

Mason throws his hands up in defeat.

"How could you do this, Mason?" Mary demands.

"What is this? Some kind of teeny-bopper intervention? I don't see what the big deal is here—"

"She's pregnant, isn't she?" Josephine says levelly.

Mason stares at them. "What?"

The triplets groan.

"We're poor, Mason, but not poor enough for you not to buy condoms."

"How could you be so irresponsible?"

"You know we can't afford to feed a pregnant girl *and* then another kid."

"What're you? Like, twelve? How do you even know about this kind of stuff?" Mason cuts them off, bewildered.

"We're *sixteen*, Mason."

"Whatever. Look, you guys. I swear to you that Sara is not pregnant. And, if she is, it wasn't me. Nineteen-year-old-virgin, I promise you." Mason holds his hands up, shaking his head.

"But I *saw* you—" Josephine starts.

"You *saw* me talking to her. Up close and personal, yes, but that's all. I haven't even kissed her yet." Mason rolls his eyes.

169

"She spent the night with you," Mary accuses.

"Yeah, she did. But all we did was sleep. No kissing, no sex. Scout's honor."

The three look at each other, shuffle their feet and mutter their apologies before slipping out the door. Mason isn't sure if he should laugh or cry, so he gets dressed instead. After putting his shirt on backwards and taking the time to fix it, he makes his way to the kitchen, his feet thumping heavily on the stairs.

He hears his younger siblings laughing and walks in, hoping for some breakfast.

The old 80's radio on the windowsill is playing softly in the background. Sara's surrounded by the kids, her back to him, pouring some batter into the frying pan. Mason leans against the doorframe, to watch her for a few seconds.

"And when do you flip them?" she asks.

"When you see the bubbles at the top!" A boy laughs.

"But not too many bubbles, or the bottom will be burnt," another advises seriously.

Someone looks around and notices him. "Oh, look, it's Mason!"

The children turn around and screech, jumping him. Mason smiles, letting the younger ones climb on him.

"'Ello?" Sara and Mason turn to see whose voice rings down the hall.

An elderly woman appears in the doorway. She has graying blonde hair, a plump body and a round, warm face. She holds her arms out, letting the children rush to her.

"Why, 'ello, doves! Where shall we go today?" she croons.

"Oh, June, I don't have to go to work today. You don't have to watch them," Mason interjects.

"Nonsense! It seems you've got company," June winks.

Mason smiles gratefully. "Thanks, June. Seriously, I don't know what we'd do without you."

June flicks her wrist at him, her eyes sparkling. "Pshaw, you'd get along fine. Anyway, we're going to the aquarium today. They're having a thirteen-and-under free day. Isn't that exciting?"

The kids cry their agreement as they pull June out the door. Mason runs his hand through his hair and turns back to Sara.

She's watching him, flour smudged on her chin, her hair falling out of a ponytail and curling around her face. She has one arm crossed over her chest, the opposite elbow positioned on her hand. The spatula dangles in her limp hand.

"So…" he takes a deep breath.

Sara seems to shake herself, smiling and turning back to the pan. He watches her flip the pancakes, crossing over and sitting at the bar.

"Who was that?" she asks.

"Her? Oh, that's June. She and my mom worked at the same diner together for years. She's retired now and she takes the kids when we have to work. She doesn't take pay or anything, so it helps us out a lot," he explains.

"Oh, that's nice of her." Sara replies. "Are you hungry?"

"Yes, actually."

"It should be done in a few seconds. Although I could be wrong. I've never cooked before," she confesses.

"This is a really nice change. Usually it's me cooking for everyone else." His mouth pulls up on one side.

"Yes, well, hopefully you won't regret it." She laughs.

They're quiet for a few brief seconds as Sara pokes at the mostly-cooked batter with the plastic spatula. Mason rests his elbows on the bar, folds his hands and places his chin on them, watching her. Neither of them needs conversation. This silence is nice, comfortable.

The radio seems to be louder the longer they remain quiet. After a few more seconds, Sara begins to sing softly. Mason can't help but feel surprised.

"You know this song?" he asks.

Sara turns slightly, looking at him from over her shoulder. "Oh, yes. I danced to it, once. About a year ago, now."

"Really?"

"Yes. I have my own routine to it, contemporary style. Gavis won't let me dance it in public."

Mason's brow creases. "Why not?"

"He says the naughty ballerina is the one that gets the crowd, at the end of the night."

Mason pulls a face, disgusted at Gavis' exploitation of Sara's body. But he can't help but think of how right Gavis is. At the end of the performance he'd attended, Mason had been simply star-struck. She drew a standing ovation, he remembers.

"You're stunning, when you dance," Mason comments.

Sara smiles down at her pan. "Thank you," she murmurs.

She slides the pancakes onto a chipped plate and spins, sliding it across the bar to him.

"Don't forget to turn off the stove."

"Oh, right."

The gas *poof*s out as she twists the knob. Sara takes the seat across from Mason, pulling her handle into her lap before sitting down. She watches him squeeze maple syrup from a woman-shaped bottle.

174

"You know," he says, his tone thoughtful. "My ma always said there are only two things in life you are never too poor to buy."

"Really?" Sara copies Mason's previous pose, but instead of placing her chin on top of her folded fingers, she rests her cheek on the back of one hand. "What are they?"

"Toilet paper and the good syrup."

Sara smiles as Mason spears two huge slivers of pancake and shoves them in his mouth. They watch each other as he chews and hacks the other pancakes into bite sized pieces.

"Want some?" he asks, his mouth still full.

She shakes her head automatically. "I can't eat."

"So you say. You also told me you can't sleep, either." He waves his sticky fork at her dismissively.

"True." She shakes her head. "I guess anything is possible, when you're around."

Mason pauses chewing, taking a second before swallowing. "Right."

He stabs a slice, chasing some syrup around before holding it out to her, his hand cupped under it.

Without hesitation, Sara leans over and pops it into her mouth.

Mason focuses on the way her lips close, the personal aspect he didn't realize came with sharing your food. It was a bad idea.

Or an extremely good one, depending on how you looked at the situation.

He clears his throat, letting the fork clatter to the table. "So, is it good, or what?"

She nods, chewing it slowly, thoughtfully. She can actually taste it, feel her stomach expanding as she swallows. "Are you going to finish those?" Sara asks.

Mason shakes his head, a smile dancing on his lips as he pushes the plate across the bar to her.

He puts his hands back under his chin to watch her finish the rest of the half-drowned pastries. When she's done, he clears his throat again, leaning back in his seat and shoving a hand through his hair.

"So, what do you want to do today?" he asks lazily.

"I don't know." She tilts her head. "What are my choices?"

Mason thinks for a second. "I don't think it'd be a good idea to spend the cash we just got. How about just going to the park? It's supposed to be a beautiful day."

"Okay." Sara smiles and stands, taking the empty plate to the sink. "When do you want to leave?"

"Um, well, I have to do a chore or two before we go. I guess I *should* do the dishes, but I hate that job. Wanna help me clean up the bedrooms instead? I'm sure my siblings have rearranged the furniture." He rolls his eyes. "I always have to push the beds around."

"Okay." Sara follows Mason upstairs and into the first bedroom. He shows her where to put the toys and they start taming the beastly mess his younger siblings have left lying around.

After a while, Mason looks over at her. "I think I've got it here. If you don't mind, you can go into the triplets' room next door. All you have to do is put the clothes away and make the beds."

"I don't mind."

Sara tosses him a ratty tiger before making her way into the hallway. She pushes open the neighboring door and takes a step inside.

The room is mostly clean, with messy beds and a large vanity covered with what can only be described as "stuff." Sara moves to the first bed, scooping up all the clothes and putting them in their labeled drawers in the dresser.

Time slips by quickly and Sara thinks of nothing but her work while she cleans. Soon, she has only the beds to make, and she starts on the job steadily, not feeling the pressure to rush. Thumping noises start up in the bedroom next door, but she feels no urge to question them.

As she finishes tucking in the last comforter and replacing the pillows, a flash catches her eyes. She looks up and sees her own reflection in the vanity mirror.

The light from the open window hits her strings perfectly, making them glare against the mirror's surface. She pauses, turning her wrist slightly and watching the light jump.

A frown touches her lips, creases her brow. Sara drops the pillow she's been holding, touching her string lightly, almost not at all. The string, impossibly strong,

178

almost metallic looking, glistens where her fingertips brush against it.

Mason walks into the room, sweating, breathing hard. "Hey, um, what'cha doing?"

"I'm wrong, aren't I?" Sara meets his gaze.

"What?"

"I told you once, I wasn't born this way. I know how people react to me. I don't know of anyone else like me. So I must not be natural. Wrong."

Mason crosses the room and sits down on the bed. Sara sits, also, mostly copying his reaction.

"I honestly don't know what to say," Mason tells her. He flops back, putting an arm behind his head and flinging one over his stomach.

"It's because I'm correct, isn't it?" she asks softly. She looks down at her hands, her hair falling into her face.

"Sort of. I mean, there isn't anyone like you, Sara. You are different." He smiles slightly. "But, if you think about it, everyone is different. No one is a clone."

"But that sort of difference is defined as normal. Mine is not."

Mason studies her. "Why is this bothering you all of a sudden?"

She looks down at her hands, twisting themselves around each other in her lap. She doesn't know what's keeping her quiet, but she can sense his impatience. He sits up slowly, his eyes on her. She feels the slight pressure of his hand on her elbow.

"Sara?" he prompts.

She takes a deep breath. "Because I don't want you to be ashamed of me."

Sara looks up, her blue eyes crystal clear and completely honest. Mason tenses in response, surprise shocking over his features.

Sara watches him twist off the bed and tug at his hair. He starts pacing tightly, his shoes thudding against the wooden floor, his dirty shoelaces untied and dragging along with his movements.

"Mason? What are you doing?" Sara asks after a while.

"I'm pacing."

"Why?"

"Because I'm worked up. You... work me up."

"I'm not familiar with this term, 'worked up.'" She tilts her head to the side slightly.

"It means I feel… upset, I guess." He stops pacing and blows out a breath.

"Oh." She twists her fingers together until they hurt. "I didn't mean to make you upset."

"Sara, you have to know something." He walks over and pulls her hands into his. "Okay?"

"Okay," she whispers.

"You're not normal. Okay? You're not. There is nothing normal about what Gavis did to you. But it's also not *your fault*." He smiles humorlessly. "I will never—*never*—be ashamed of you. Just because you're different more literally than figuratively doesn't mean that I'm ashamed of you. Promise me you won't doubt me about that."

"But I—"

"*Promise me.*"

Sara's breath catches. She isn't sure why, but it must have something to do with the ferocity of Mason's tone, the sincerity in his eyes. She feels her own fingers tighten around his.

"I promise."

×××

Sara stands with her feet crossed over each other, cradling a smooth stone in her hands. She looks out across the water, glimpsing tiny moments in other people's lives. A group of girls swimming around on the other side, some older men fishing, a young couple riding bikes together and a girl sitting on a bench playing an acoustic guitar for cash. She sees it all, wonders at their expressions and rolls the stone over and over in her hands.

She looks over at the guitar playing girl. "Her voice is very pleasing."

Mason looks up at her from his spot on the ground before leaning around to see the other girl. He watches her for a few moments until his gaze comes back to Sara.

"You like it?" he asks.

"No. I mean, I can't."

Mason halfheartedly chucks a rock into the lake. "How do you know it's pleasing, then?"

"Almost everyone who walks by puts money in her case. And you were humming along with her earlier." Sara looks down at him. "The lyrics are creative. She's quite clever."

"Yeah, I like it," Mason agrees.

Sara doesn't respond. She opens her hands a little to look down at her rock. She smoothes her thumb over it several times, marveling at the sensation of it. She's still trying to get used to feeling everything she touches and readapting herself to human life. She wants to hold onto the rock but doesn't understand why. She follows Mason's example and tosses it into the pond. She watches the ripples come back and whisper against the bank before she turns away.

She sits down next to Mason, leaning into him. He accepts the weight of her and clears his throat. She can feel him tense a little where she touches him.

"So you can't feel emotions yet?" he asks.

She hesitates for a second, thinking. "No. Have you ever seen fish swimming under ice?"

"What? No," he replies. He's obviously confused by her statement, his brow creased.

"Fish that live in deep bodies of water can live even in the dead of winter. Even though the top of the water freezes, sometimes so much that a human can stand on it safely, the bottom of the water stays liquid. The fish swim down there, so they can survive the cold," she explains. "It's kind of like that."

He shakes his head. "I don't know what you're talking about."

"It's like I'm standing on top of the ice and I'm looking down at the fish. I am aware of their presence, I can almost touch them, but they lie beneath the surface, just out of reach." She takes one of his hands in hers and considers it briefly. "You know, Gavis is afraid of you. He realizes that whenever I'm with you, everything about my life before him comes rushing back. When you leave, those feelings shrink away again and I relapse."

"I want you to feel," Mason replies softly.

"I do, too."

They fall silent. Sara keeps her eyes on his hand pressed into both of hers. She runs her fingertips over several scars, inspecting every centimeter of this small

184

piece of him. It hints of a story, one that she wants to hear, to know and to memorize. Almost reflexively, she pulls his hand up to her face and presses a kiss to his palm.

He shakes his hand loose of her and moves it to the side of her face instead. He gently turns her head to look at him. She meets his eyes and really sees him for the first time.

Broad forehead covered with a mess of dark hair. Two wide, dark eyes with just a hint of green in them, depthless and emotive. A smallish button nose and a few light freckles sprinkled over high cheek bones and nose. Full lips, with the top one slightly smaller than the bottom, currently pulled up in what can only be described as a sad smile.

He's studying her, too, she notices, and not for the first time, she wonders what he sees there. She wonders what he's thinking as his eyes move ever so slightly to take her in. She wonders if he finds her beautiful.

"I know you can't feel the same way," he says quietly. "But I love you, you know?"

His eyes shut as he leans in and kisses her mouth.

Sara closes her eyes as well. The only thing she feels is his lips against hers, slightly chapped and completely gentle. She feels herself relax further into him in response and notes how everything inside of her has seemed to freeze.

Then, like a bubble popping, they're all there. They fill her from her toes up, and they wreak chaos in her soul. They fill her stomach with butterflies, shoot heat through her chest. She lets out a little gasp automatically.

Mason starts to pull away, but she surges up, pressing more firmly against his mouth. He submits, and kisses her more fervently this time.

She's shocked, she's overjoyed, she's thrilled and terrified and confused. She's riding a rollercoaster that no one else can see or hear, but it's all she knows and all she wants to know.

But when Mason sits back, she lets him. She opens her eyes and looks at his face, so fiercely beautiful to her now. She sees the new light in his eyes, the color rising to his cheeks. She can make out a dark line on his bottom lip where he bit down, or maybe she bit him?

She can't remember, but it's so unimportant to her now. His expression becomes concerned.

"Sara?"

She feels like she's a cork bobbing on the top of a new and exciting ocean. She can't find words to speak, so she just shakes her head sharply. This only upsets him more.

"Sara, are you alright?"

Her breath hitches like she might cry and she shakes her head again.

"You're *not* alright?" His sharp tone makes her wince a little. "I stepped over some boundary, didn't I?"

She sees the self hate well up in his eyes, and that wonderful light there extinguishes. He looks away from her and mutters a curse, moving to get to his feet.

Her hand reaches out and grips his upper arm. He looks down at it, surprised, before looking back to her.

She swallows and takes a deep breath. "Mason?"

"Yeah?" He's wary of her now.

"I know you told me I can't feel the same way," she replies slowly. "But I do. I love you, Mason. With all my heart I do."

This stuns him. She watches him process it, a new kind of hope burning in his gaze. "Do you mean...?"

"Yes, Mason. I—I feel again."

Part Six

Abby hesitates at the door of a very old flower shop. No one with magic ever makes her tense, but the girl she's going to see is powerful in a different way. This girl, though her physical powers are worlds weaker than Abby's, has the gift of life.

The door opens before Abby can reach out and take hold of the handle. A man stands there, his eyes quickly taking her in. He's taller than she is, with short black cropped hair, dark sunglasses, a white t-shirt, jeans, and dark, patent leather shoes. She notes with relief the leather gloves that are pulled over his hands.

"Zalia," he says, surprised.

"I go by Abana now, John," she replies. "Or Abby, if you prefer."

He leans against the doorway, crossing his arms over his chest. "What are you doing here?"

"I came to see her," Abby says.

He's quiet for a long moment, his lips pursed together. Abby shifts nervously as some birds land on the windowsill near them. She glances over at the chattering animals before looking back at John.

"She's not here," he says finally. "She's at her place up on the west side. Got a migraine yesterday and I haven't heard from her since. A vision, I think, but you already know that. It's why you're here, isn't it? You only come around when you need her."

Abby feels shame heat her face. "John—"

"I told you where to find her. That's all I'm doing for you," he snaps. "You were *so* much help to us the last time."

Her eyes immediately go to his gloved hands. They're balled into tight fists, and she knows it's not just because he's angry with her.

"Just go, Zalia," he says, softer this time. "Or Abby, if *you* prefer."

He turns away and shuts the door. She stands there for a few more seconds, staring at the old wood.

"I'm sorry," she whispers dejectedly.

She vanishes from the doorway, but reappears quickly in front of a beautiful building somewhere on the west side.

×××

Mason pauses at the bottom of the steps, shaking his head.

"Are you sure you don't want to, I don't know, *do* something?" he asks. "I mean, you've just gotten your emotions back."

Sara, already on the second step, looks down at him. She squeezes his fingers, laced in hers and smiles. "I'm with you," she replies. "I *am* doing something."

"I guess." He shakes his head again but lets her drag him up the stairs. He keeps an eye out for her strings; he's terrified of stepping on them. "I just wouldn't think this is the place you'd want to be."

"Wherever you are is where I want to be."

Mason rolls his eyes. Still, he can't suppress his smile. He's not really into the sappy lovey-dovey crap most people call romance, but coming from Sara, it just seems natural. She's saying exactly what she's thinking exactly when she thinks it.

Mason follows Sara through the door, shutting it with his foot. "I guess I can say the same for you," he says.

She wraps her arms around his neck, leaning into him. Mason lets her push him back until he's resting against the door. He puts his arms around her middle.

"You mean it?" she asks.

"I mean it."

It's so strange to him now, seeing her happy expression and knowing she really means it. But his feelings for her aren't any different now that she's changed. She just seems more like Sara.

Sara, on the other hand, can hardly contain herself. Everything's new and exciting and filled with Love, like the edges of her vision are tainted pink. She wonders if she'd float away if Mason weren't here to tether her down.

She puts her hand to his face, placing her thumb on the corner of his mouth. She watches him smile, raise an eyebrow. He's enjoying this, she can tell. He's enjoying letting her be in control, do what she wants.

She smiles back and then presses their mouths together. His hand comes up to tangle in her hair as they kiss, and she's more than happy. She wants this to last forever, just the two of them. She wants him all to herself.

Eventually they come up for air, but Sara ducks her head, to kiss up his neck softly. She ends up at his ear, and she plants a kiss there, as well.

"I want to go to your room," she whispers.

"Oh, really?"

She loves the slow way he says it, the chuckle that follows. She can feel it slide down her spine, and she shivers, delightedly.

"Yes really," she replies. "Please, Mason? Please?"

He's quiet for so long she pulls back to see his expression. She can see that his eyes seem darker and his smile has turned impish. He looks at her for a few more seconds before he tilts her head down and presses his lips to her forehead.

"Okay," he says against her skin.

She bounces in place, grinning, before pulling him towards the stairs. He laughs and stumbles behind her; the two of them practically run down the hall.

Mason catches her when they reach his bedroom. Laughing, she kisses him again, enchanted by the way it makes her feel. Her toes curl automatically. She loves this. She loves him.

He pushes her back a step or two between kisses, letting his hands creep up to her waist. She hardly notices, her mind too focused on what his mouth is doing.

Suddenly, his hands tighten, and he picks her up. Yelping in surprise, she kicks once before he tosses her onto the bed. She flounders in the sheets and pillows for a few seconds before resurfacing, her hair a tousled mess. She pushes it out of her face, her eyes wide.

"You threw me on the bed!" she shouts.

Mason grins, leaning on the bedpost. "Why, yes. Yes I did. What are you going to do about it?"

She stares at him, shocked. Her mind races, thinking up a response, any response to give him.

He inclines his head a bit. "Well?"

She palms a pillow under her hand before lifting it up. She draws it back and quickly hits him with it.

It's his turn to be surprised. He looks at her, bewildered as she raises it to hit him again, a smug smile settling on her lips. She flings it toward him.

He's ready for it this time, and he catches it, deftly twisting it out of her hands. She shrieks as he drops it on the floor and lunges for her. She dives for another pillow weapon, but he grabs her by the waist, taking her down.

"No you don't," he growls. "Fool me once, shame on you."

She laughs, squirming around in his arms. She manages to grab another pillow and starts hitting him with it awkwardly. He sits up, attempting to take it from her, but she catches him square in the face. He automatically jerks back and falls off the bed.

"Mason?" Sara sits up quickly, her tone worried. He doesn't answer. "Mason?"

He pops over the lip of the bed, the other pillow in his hand. He sends it sailing at her face, catching her off guard.

"Gotcha!" he crows.

"That's not fair!" she objects. She hits him as he tries to stand up. "You cheated!"

"I did not!"

"You did too!"

Mason jumps on the bed, to get the advantage, and Sara stands, as well. They hit each other a few more times, laughing, before Mason is able to knock the pillow from her hands. He tosses his own weapon off the bed. Sara tries to catch her breath from all the laughing. She sits down and flops on her back.

He grins, sitting next to her. "I won."

"You cheated!"

"Well, you know what they say."

Sara looks up at him, shaking her head. She looks into his eyes, waiting for him to go on. "I don't know."

"All's fair in love and war," he says.

This brings a brilliant smile to her flushed face. "Love?"

Mason slides down, propping himself up on his elbow. "Yeah, I guess." He winks.

"Please say it, Mason."

"I don't know if I want to now," he confesses. "Now that you asked me, it just seems… less."

"Less?" Sara brow creases. "Less what?"

"Less meaningful, I guess." He shrugs.

"I still want to hear it." She brushes some hair off his forehead.

One side of his mouth pulls up and he brings their faces closer together. "I love you, Sara."

"I love you, too," she says.

She presses their lips together once more, and feels him smiling through the kiss. She presses close to him, wanting to feel more, marveling in the intensity of it all. His hand comes up to cup her face, and she lets him tilt her head back.

Sara's eyes open at the ring of an unfamiliar sound. She breaks the kiss, sitting up.

"What was that?" she asks.

Mason leans over and kisses her shoulder softly. "Your stomach growled. You must be hungry."

Sara looks down at her middle, putting a hand there. The sound comes again, along with the feeling that something's moving around inside her.

"Hungry," she repeats slowly. "It's different than I remember."

Mason rolls off the bed, onto his feet. He laces his fingers and holds them over his head. Sara watches his shirt lift as he stretches, revealing a strip of skin. She smiles involuntarily.

"Want anything in particular?" he groans.

"I don't know," she replies.

He drops his arms. "A sandwich it is, then."

He leans down to kiss her forehead before he pads out into the hallway. She watches him go, waiting until he's out of sight before flopping back onto his bed. She toes the sheets, smiling to herself. After a few quiet moments, she flips over and presses her nose to the blanket, taking a deep breath. It smells like Mason, a scent that can't be described as anything but him.

She pushes herself up on her elbows and looks around. She didn't really notice anything this morning, not like she's noticing it now. Untangling herself from her strings, she gets off the bed. Sara wanders over to his dresser, covered with bills and old notes from his sisters.

She moves around his room slowly, taking everything in. The floorboards creak under the weight of her bare feet. She clasps her hands behind her back, her handle hitting the floor softly.

201

There really isn't much to look at, which tells her more than anything. But as bare as it is, it fits him perfectly. She imagines him sitting on the bed during his days off, just closing his eyes and listening to the chaos downstairs. This little space of cleanliness must seem like a safe haven for him.

She stops at the stacks of books against the back wall, looking down curiously.

She looks back at the door and sees nothing. She debates going downstairs to join him, but after a glance at the pile of novels, she decides against it. Sara folds her legs under her, and sits Indian style in front of them.

She runs her fingers over the titles on a few of the spines. There are some old philosophy books there, and she remembers back to the first time they met.

There are a few old classics, nothing new. She's surprised to find a book by Emily Brontë; she remembers it used to be her mother's favorite. She can remember a time when her mother was having a good day and they'd sit on the porch, her mother reading out loud while Sara played with her old doll.

Sara finishes looking at the selection on his floor, and she turns towards the dresser, placing one hand on a stack to help her stand. She stops as she glances at the space between the dresser and the wall.

There seems to be a book wedged there, covered in dust without a title on the spine. It looks as if it belongs with the other books. It's bound with cracked leather, and an ornate design decorates the side. She hesitates, looking to the door again. He's not there and she can't hear him. She reaches out and grips the book.

It takes some time to coax out—it's jammed that tightly—but she manages to free it. She sits back down, setting it on her lap. She disturbs the layer of grime on the cover, not finding any markings to identify it. Carefully, she lifts the cover.

It's not a book at all: it's a photo album. The first picture is of a small, red-faced baby. Inked in the corner is simply, *Mason—May 21st*.

She touches the writing briefly, staring at the tiny child that was once Mason. The picture below it is of a very young girl—Mason's mother—in a hospital bed, holding the baby. A man stands beside her, his arms crossed, looking directly into the camera instead of at his child. He looks so similar to Mason, it's almost disturbing. He looks no older than Mason is now.

Sara turns the page and comes across an ocean of old pictures. Ones of Mason as a child, other children and Anita. But only an occasional glimpse of Mason's father, always wearing the same cold expression. His dark eyes, otherwise identical to Mason's, hold none of Mason's warmth or passion.

The album is stuffed full of these captured moments, these still frames that piece together the story of a sad little boy in an unhappy household surrounded by stress and darkness all the time. Even when the other kids are smiling brightly into the camera, Mason hangs back, his own expression forced, uncomfortable.

The last page in the book has just one picture. It's of Mason, and was obviously taken a few years ago. He's standing outside the house, in a t-shirt, jeans, and Converse. His arms are crossed over his chest, his hair is a little shaggier, and he's a few inches shorter as well. He's not even trying to smile here, his face a cold, calculating mask his like father's. Sara lets her mind blur the line between Mason and his father just for a second and realizes that she can hardly see a difference between the two.

She hears heavy footsteps in the hall, and Mason walks into the room, a plate balanced on both of his upturned palms.

"I made two sandwiches," he says. "Just in case you don't like one or the other."

Sara twists her body, tilting her chin to look up at him. "I found this."

Mason finally notices what she's holding and stops. He stares at it for a few long seconds before bending down and sliding a plate across the floor to her. It stops just beside her knee.

"Haven't seen that in a while," he says. He backs up and sits on the bed, staring down at his own plate.

"You look like your father," Sara says.

"I know."

Mason frowns down at his own sandwich before setting it on the bed beside him. Sara watches him blow out a breath, run a hand through his hair. She feels guilty, like she's done something wrong.

205

"I didn't mean to upset you," she says. She can feel unhappiness rise in her like a thermometer in the desert.

His eyes flash to her. "You didn't."

He gets off the bed, kneeling beside her. She reaches out to him, lets him take her in his arms. She feels comforted for the moment, though that twinge of guilt still lingers.

He holds her gently for a minute or two. Then he kisses the top of her head and leans back, picking up the plate. He pushes it into her hands, deftly removing the photo album and closing it. He tosses it aside, clearing his throat.

"Eat," he advises. "I didn't make it for nothing."

She picks it up, looking it over curiously. "What is it?"

"Tuna, sweet pickles, mayo and salt," he says. "Go on, try it. It's good."

"It smells weird." She holds it away from her nose.

"It smells like fish." He rolls his eyes.

She takes a bite, rolling it around in her mouth for a bit. She scrunches her face, spitting it back out onto the plate.

Mason laughs, leaning back on his hands. "Gross! Why didn't you swallow it?"

"Because it tastes bad!" Sara cries.

She shoves the plate onto his lap, her nose still wrinkled disdainfully. She can still feel the tuna flavor coating the inside of her mouth.

Mason shakes his head, grabbing the other plate off his bed. He hands it to her.

"Try that instead," he says. "It's ham, mustard, cheese and lettuce. Even Marcy likes it, which is really saying something."

Sara picks it up, eyeing it even more carefully than the last time. She sniffs it. It doesn't seem too terrible to her. She lifts the top layer of bread, looking at the food lying inside.

"Don't be such a girl," Mason teases. "Just try it."

She sticks her tongue out at him before taking a tiny bite. She chews it over thoughtfully, her stomach growling in response.

"Well?" Mason asks around a mouthful of tuna. He waves the unwanted sandwich at her. "What do you think?"

"I like it," she replies. She takes a larger bite, more confident now. He nods.

They eat in silence for a while. Sara lets her eyes wander around his room again, trying to take in every detail. She finds it harder to do now, because her emotions seem to be distracting her. They don't allow her to see anything objectively.

"Why don't you like talking about your father?" she asks.

Mason looks at her. He's been looking around, as well, and she has caught him off guard. He swallows; his brow furrows.

"There aren't very many happy memories that go along with him," he says. He fleetingly glances at the discarded book. "Besides, it's not something we talk about any more."

"Why not?"

"Some things are better left unsaid," he explains. "No one really likes to even think about it. It's like a terrible secret everyone knows about but no one wants to address."

"That's awful," Sara says.

"Yeah," he agrees. "But it's just something we live with. We all deal with it in our own ways."

Sara stares at him a while, her clear eyes serious. She tilts her head a little, considering him. "Just because you look like him doesn't mean you are—or could be—him," she says.

Mason opens his mouth to reply but is interrupted by a sharp knock from downstairs. He twists around, looking out into the hallway, a puzzled expression settling on his face.

"Who could that be?" he mutters. "No one we know ever knocks."

He turns back, looking at Sara. "Stay here."

He puts his plate aside, standing up. Sara waits until he's at the bedroom door before scrambling to her feet. She scampers after him, ignoring his stern look.

"I have a bad feeling about this," she whispers. She twists her strings around her hands.

He starts down the hall. "So do I."

As they head down the stairs, Mason gestures Sara to stop a few steps from the bottom. She does, her hands fluttering on the banister nervously. Mason puts a hand on the door and pulls it open without hesitating.

The gray fedora lifts as Gavis looks up, his green eyes livid.

"Do you normally keep guests waiting this long?" Gavis asks, concerned. "It's really quite rude, you know."

"You're no guest," Mason snarls. He closes the door a bit, leaning against the frame.

"Well, in that case, I'll just be collecting Sara, and we'll be on our way." He gestures to the door. "If you think you're keeping me from seeing her, it's too late. You should never have opened the door."

"You can't have her," Mason says. "She isn't yours."

"The fact of the matter is, she's not yours, either. I don't see your *name* on her anywhere," Gavis mocks.

"I don't see yours either."

"No, but you do see strings." Gavis smirks, adjusting the hat on his head. "I've tired of this juvenile exchange already. Just give her to me and we'll be out of your unruly hair for good."

210

"No," Mason says stubbornly.

Gavis suppresses a sigh, his eyes flashing. "Sara, shall we end this now?"

Sara pads down the stairs, wringing her hands. She steps behind Mason, standing on her toes to see Gavis. Mason looks over his shoulder at her, reluctantly opening the door wider.

"Hello, dear," Gavis smiles at her. "Are you ready to go?"

"I don't want to go," Sara replies. "I love him."

"Aw, I know. But we'll be leaving directly, pet, and you'll forget about him, I promise."

Mason shakes his head. "Sara, I—"

"Sara," Gavis interrupts. "I know that you're upset with me now. I know you don't want to come with me. But I also know that you're excited to tell me about what else you're feeling. I know that you want to believe me about forgetting this boy. You know that this can only end one way."

Sara wavers. He's right, of course. She does know that Gavis will win, no matter what. How long it will take and who else will get hurt in the process are the

211

only variables. She looks up at Mason, suddenly afraid for him.

Mason looks at her, disbelief coloring his features. "Sara."

"Yes, Sara. You understand how this will pan out," Gavis says. "Come along, now. We have much to discuss."

Sara tries to memorize Mason's face in the short time she has, her heart beating heavily in her chest. She finally looks down, stepping out of the doorway, closer to Gavis.

Mason grabs her arm as she slips past him. "Sara, no."

"I have to go, Mason," she says. "I have to. Don't you see?"

"Yes, boy, you really have no idea who you're dealing with." Gavis examines his fingernails absently.

"Sara, I—"

"Please. Let me go."

Mason stares at her for a long second, taking in her expression. She wonders what he sees there, feeling her sadness well up to wet her eyes. She sees his expression fall flat, and his hand drops from her arm numbly. He looks older than she's ever seen him now. This makes her even sadder.

She turns back to Gavis. He offers her his hand, just like he did all those years ago in her mother's sinking car. And history repeats itself as her fingers slip into his and they vanish from Mason's doorstep.

Mason takes a step out to where the pair has just been. He stands there for a long time until his legs feel like they might give out on him. He stumbles to the first step, sitting down on it.

He wants to be angry, to scream and throw things and find strength to be brave and rescue Sara in a blaze of glory and determination. Instead he feels nothing but hollowness. He wonders if this is what Sara felt like all those years.

A wind picks up around him, spinning a thin coat of purple powder across the stoop.

He turns, frowning at the tattered woman behind him, with wild hair and crazed purple eyes. Her breathing is erratic, harsh.

213

"You couldn't have come, like, twenty minutes earlier?" Mason smiles sardonically.

"She's been taken, then?" Abby gasps.

Mason's smile drops like the woman slapped it off. "Wait, you *knew* he was coming? You knew and you didn't *warn us*?"

"Look, we don't have much time—"

"No, *you* look. I thought you were on our side—"

"Shut. Up. For one second, *shut your mouth.*"

Mason's stunned into silence. He sits back in his chair, taking in Abby's furious glare. She looks like she's been through hell.

"I'm not the Abby you know. Well, I am, but I don't know about this yet." She blows out a breath at his puzzled expression. "I'm not explaining this very clearly. I'm from two days in the future."

"Why are you here?" Mason asks. He stands.

"I want to know what you'd be willing to do to save her."

"Anything." Mason's voice is as level as his gaze.

"Seriously consider it, Mason. Think of your family, of your life here. Would you be willing to risk it

all? What if you were never be able to return here?"
Abby asks.

Mason takes a little more time to think. "Yes."

"Alright. I'm going to tell you what you have to do.
But, first, there are some things Sara has to know—
things you'll have to tell her."

"Okay."

"Things like her mother is still alive, and how to
call '911,' and how to use this phone."

Mason scrambles to catch the cellular Abby tosses
at him. "But—"

"Time, Mason, time! Tomorrow you'll go through
the park. Bring nothing but that cell phone—don't
forget it, no matter what, it's important now. You'll
meet a girl and she'll give you some advice; she's
expecting you. Then you'll go to Sara's apartment..."

Part Seven

Mason's shoes find their way on the park's path. He waits for a girl he's never seen. He sticks his hands deep into his pockets, his face downcast, and watches his feet carrying him onward.

The sound of laughter causes him to look up. Down the path, a young couple sits on a bench. They sit at almost opposite sides, but their hands meet in the middle, touching softly. The boy is dressed in a white v-neck t-shirt, jeans, and plain black shoes. She's dressed just as simply: her hair is pulled up in an uncomplicated bun, and she's wearing a white cotton dress, and a modest amount of jewelry. A pair of gladiator sandals are tossed carelessly beside an acoustic guitar that lies in the grass by their feet.

The boy glances up once and then again until he's staring at Mason. He says something Mason can't hear, and nods towards him. The girl turns around, her eyes zeroing in on him. She smiles, keeping her eyes on Mason even as her friend stands up. Mason walks towards them.

"I've been waiting for you," she says.

The boy drops her hand, but doesn't move away. He assesses Mason silently.

"Is this him?" he asks.

She waves her hand at him. "Obviously. We should be done soon."

Mason shifts uncomfortably under the other man's stare, sensing that he isn't as plain as he seems to be. Eventually, the other boy drops his gaze, looking back at the girl before turning and walking away.

"Have a seat, Mason," the girl says. She pats the empty bench next to her and looks up.

Mason does what she asks, not feeling any more at ease than before the other boy left. He rubs his hands on his jeans, clearing his throat. He notes a bouquet of flowers lying on the bench next to the girl.

She picks them up, twirling them around in her fingers gently. She tips her head, pushing her nose in the middle of them.

"Don't mind him. He's been a little difficult lately," she says.

"Why?"

She lays the flowers on her lap, passing her fingers over them until she finds one she likes. Mason watches her pick it up to inspect it. The leaves are brown and curling, the stem wilted.

"It's a long story… a *very* long story." She smiles to herself, smirking at some unknown joke. "One I have no interest in telling you."

"Oh," Mason drops the conversation awkwardly. "So, how do you know my name?"

She gives him a strange look. "I saw this coming, of course. And Zalia came to see me. Didn't she tell you anything?"

"You mean Abby? No, she didn't say anything except I was supposed to meet you here."

The girl shakes her head, looking up at the sky. "She makes everything so complicated. It's a wonder I put up with it."

"Look, I don't want to be rude, but I'm kind of in a hurry," Mason interrupts. "What's your name?"

"You only think you're in a hurry." The girl raises an eyebrow. "Call me Mo."

"Mo," he repeats slowly.

"Fo sho." She smirks. "I am roughly two hundred years old, I'm clairvoyant and slightly psychic."

"Aren't they the same thing?" he asks.

She waves her hand dismissively. "Not at all. Clairvoyant is simply knowing things about a person that no one else knows. Like how I know you come from a single parent family and used to have a girlfriend named April Caine. Being psychic is when you see glimpses of the future."

"And you're only slightly psychic?"

"I can see about fifteen minutes into the future. I have had a couple long term visions, one of them including this conversation, but that's extremely rare." She shrugs. "I can also do this."

To demonstrate, she gives him the flower she's been holding. What was once on the verge of dying now looks freshly cut. It is a healthy green, its petals an unnatural shade of blue.

"We can't all have pretty purple magic." She shrugs.

"Huh." Mason stares at the flower. "That's pretty cool."

222

She looks away, putting her bare feet on top of the guitar shyly. "I'd like to think so."

"How is this supposed to help me?" Mason asks.

"Well—" she pauses dramatically. "—I'm not exactly sure."

Mason drops the flower on the bench. "Okay then."

He attempts to stand, but she grabs his wrist and pulls him back. "Slow your roll, Captain Ahab."

"What are you talking about?" he demands.

"Captain Ahab is a crucial character in Melville's novel *Moby Dick* and—"

Mason shakes his head impatiently. "I get the reference. But that doesn't make any sense."

"I made it up right now, thanks," she replies smoothly. "And if you decide to be less of a dick, maybe we can sit down like grownups and discuss your situation."

The irritation rushes out of Mason as he looks down into her amused expression. He sits down docilely, running a hand over his face.

"Sorry," he says. "I'm just a little stressed out."

"Really? I couldn't tell." She grins brightly.

"Mason, you need to realize that everything happens in due time. You just have to be patient."

"It's hard," he admits.

"Believe me, I know," she snorts. "Especially with a soul mate waiting on the other line."

"You know about soul mates?" he asks.

His surprised tone makes her smile. She points to something over his shoulder. Mason turns around and sees her friend standing at a candy cart down the path.

"That's him," she says. "He's the love of my life."

"So what am I supposed to do?" Mason asks.

Mo looks around, as if searching for something. She points to herself, looking back at him. "Are you talking to me?"

"Of course I am!" he says. "Who else would I be talking to?"

"Well, I don't know. But why are you asking me what you should be doing? Isn't that something you should be figuring out for yourself?"

"Why am I even here talking to you? How is this going to help me?" Mason demands impatiently.

224

"All in good time, love, all in good time." She stretches. "Maybe you're here to learn some *patience*. You can't run into this half cocked. You need a plan, a carefully devised scheme, if you will. And, preferably, something that will work."

"How do you know what I'm running into?"

She looks at him from the corner of her eye. "I'm slightly psychic, remember? I had a vision. I know what you're doing."

"And you can't tell me anything?" he repeats.

He watches her tilt her head, wisps of loose hair curling around her face. She moves her feet on top of the guitar, tracing invisible patterns with her toes. She smoothes her dress down.

Mason can't help but notice her simple beauty, so similar to Abby's. He wonders if it's because of how young she looks, so fresh and full of life, when her real age is incredible. It's the way they carry themselves, he thinks—the slight lift in their shoulders, the ancient look in their eyes. They're just different.

She looks back at him, oblivious to his scrutinizing gaze. "I can tell you one thing."

He waits for a second, waiting for her to say more. "Well?"

"Not everyone gets a happy ending." She blows out a breath, looking away. "Do you see those two boys over there? They both have really dark hair."

Mason swivels around, catching sight of two guys his age. They're standing quite a bit away, next to an antique-looking motorcycle. "Yeah, I see them."

"The one on the left is the *other* love of my life."

Mason turns back, to see her half hearted smile. "But I thought you have a soul mate?"

"I do," she replies quickly. "But the heart has more than enough room for love. I love them both, you see, but one will always trump the other. We were in love and I left him. It's the way it has to be sometimes. One love leaves for a better purpose and the other must accept that."

"She's not going to understand," he says. "Sara, I mean. She's going to fight as hard as she can."

Mo reaches over and places her hand on top of Mason's. "As she should. No one ever wants someone to go, even when there's a good enough reason. She'll come to understand, though. She has to."

"I think it's time," a voice says.

Both Mason and Mo look up. The other boy—the one she called her soul mate—is standing on the path, a giant bag of cotton candy in one hand. He looks at Mason and smiles slightly.

"Your soul mate," he continues. "She's waiting for you."

Mo draws back, rubbing her hands on her dress. "Good luck, Mason."

"Thanks."

Mason stands, nodding at the boy. He steps onto the path, walking away from the couple, towards Gavis and Sara. He thinks about what Mo's told him, about needing a plan that will work. He has a suspicion he already knows what he has to do.

"Mason!"

He turns, just in time to catch a flying body in his arms.

Mo hugs him fiercely, and whispers in his ear. "Everything works out the way it should, in the end.

227

Even if it's not the way you want it to be, or not what you expect, it's how it should be. Remember that."

He nods and lets her go. She puts her hands on his shoulders, looking into his eyes with her electric gaze. Finally, she lets him go and steps back, a smile spreading across her lips.

"Go get 'em, Tiger," she says.

×××

Sara struggles against the handcuff. Tears continue to spill out of the corners of her eyes, but she tries to keep her sobs to a minimum. She doesn't want to upset Gavis.

"Sara, I told you before, if you don't try to run away, I'll unlock you. But I can't risk you leaving again."

She turns her wet face up to see him. Gavis rests against the counter she's locked to, remorse tainting his expression. His only response from her is a choked sob.

"Come now, it's not so bad." His eyes soften.

"Why can't I be with Mason?" she asks.

Gavis sighs. "Mason this, Mason that. You see, Sara, it's illegal for me to tamper with humans, like I did with you and the others before you. If I let you roam about, people will come to realize what I did and then I'll be killed. It's a witch hunt world out there, don't you get that?"

"Because of my strings?"

"Because of your strings." He nods.

"Why can't you just take them off?"

"Because I don't know how," he barks.

She watches through blurry eyes as his eyes flash green before he seems to calm himself. He unknots his fists, pushing away from the counter and walks around the lopsided table, stuffing his fingers deep into his white-washed jeans pockets.

"I don't want you to be afraid of me, Sara," Gavis says in a low voice.

"I'm not." She wipes the tears from her eyes with the back of her free hand.

Gavis continues his pacing. "I know. Please understand that I don't want you to be unhappy. Everything I've ever done has been to protect you."

"Mason doesn't think so," Sara replies.

"*Mason*—" Gavis chokes off the last bit of his sentence.

Sara cringes away from his tone, his voice, his impeccably green, fiery eyes. She watches his hands curl and shake, his fists start to glow an alarming jade color.

He spins away from her, yanking on his hair; a very Mason thing to do. "You don't understand, Sara. Emotions destroy people. Emotions are the reason people steal, murder, covet. I was trying to protect you by taking them away, trying to give you a chance at a decent life. I've been trying to do so ever since because I like you."

"You like me, but Mason loves me," Sara replies evenly. "Gavis, why won't you let me go? Why can't you just let me be with him?"

"Because, eventually, he will hurt you. They all do." Gavis sighs, tossing his hands up. "I'm done arguing with you. I'll be back soon."

As Gavis evaporates, leaving behind a sparkling ivy curtain, Sara wipes the remaining tears from her face. She tugs halfheartedly on the handcuff, knowing there's no chance she'll get free. She feels older than she is in this moment. Sara scrubs her free hand over her face, giving up.

The door rattles.

Sara lets out a breathless squeak, cowering against the cheap faux-wood. She knows it's not Gavis; he would simply materialize.

The frame shakes again but it's locked. Everything goes silent for a few seconds and Sara holds her breath.

The door jumps suddenly as someone slams a foot under the knob. This goes on for a few more seconds and then stops once more.

As the apartment goes still, Sara releases her breath. Whoever it was must have given up. Silence reigns for about five minutes, except for a lonely clock that ticks tiredly, skipping beats every now and again.

Suddenly, the door explodes inward. Sara screams as she is showered in slivers of wood.

"Oh, my God. Oh, my God that hurt." Mason lays sprawled, clutching his right shoulder. "That was a terrible idea. I think I broke it. Holy shit."

"*Mason*?" Sara yelps.

He rolls onto his knees, putting his forehead on the floor and groaning, "Just give me a second."

She's too shocked to do anything but stare at him. Adrenaline courses through her veins.

Mason staggers to his feet. "Never do anything you've seen in a movie."

"Are you telling me or speaking rhetorically?" Sara asks.

"Doesn't matter." Mason grabs the handcuff and braces his foot against the cupboard. He leans away, tugging on the metal.

The screws groan in protest, but he gets nowhere. He quickly abandons the attempt, kneeling down by her.

"Mason," Sara whispers. She cups his face in her free hand.

"Hey, no time. You gotta stay with me." Mason takes a phone from his pocket and holds in front of her eyes. "You need this. Hide it."

"Where?" She pulls it from his grasp.

"Anywhere. Sit on it if you have to." He slips his long fingers under her chin, forcing her gaze back to his. "Gavis lied. You're mother's still alive."

Sara's breathing stops for so long, she wonders if she ever really breathed in the first place. "What?"

"When I tell you, you take out that phone and dial '911'. Got it?"

"But Mason—"

"Repeat the number back to me, Sara." Mason's eyes are grave.

She hesitates but obliges. He blows out a breath, sitting back on his heels. She sticks the phone in a fold of her dress as she watches him rub his palms against his denim pants.

"No matter what happens, I love you, okay?" His gaze is steady but troubled. "No matter what I say or do, it's all for you. You know that right?"

"Mason, what's going on?" Sara's voice trembles.

"I never believed in soul mates until I met you. It's crazy isn't it?" His eyes take on a sort of strange gleam.

"Mason—"

Mason kisses her roughly, and Sara can feel pent up tension in his jaw. It feels too desperate, too edged out for her to feel comfortable. She turns away.

"Mason, you're scaring me."

He twists, standing. He starts to pace, hands on his hips. He checks his watch, muttering to himself. Sara catches the word 'patience' several times. She tugs at the handcuff more forcefully this time.

Gavis reappears, waving some green sparkles away. "Sara, the new place is—"

He stops, eyes narrowing at the sight of Mason. "Really?"

"Yes." Mason leans back on his heels, hands curling into fists.

Gavis looks around, his eyes widening when he catches sight of the mess. "You broke my door," he says. His tone is full of disbelief.

"Well, the fire escape is out of order. It was the only way to get in," Mason explains.

"You couldn't have knocked like a civilized person?" Gavis cries. "For heaven's sake, I have to pay for that!"

"Are we really going to argue about the door? Aren't there more important things to yell about?" Mason asks.

"Be quiet," Gavis snaps. "I'm still trying to wrap my head around the fact that you *demolished my door while breaking into my apartment.* Do you have any idea how much a door costs these days?"

"Around a thousand dollars," Mason replies.

Gavis stares at him, pulling on the brim of his hat gently. "You know that for a fact?"

"I work at Sven's, remember? We fix doors all the time. That's a pretty plain door but if you want to buy a new one for the resale value of the apartment, you're going to have to go a little pricier."

"Huh." Gavis seems to think this over. "A thousand dollars, eh?"

"Around that."

Sara holds her breath as the two are silent for a moment or two. Mason shifts awkwardly. Gavis stares at the door, a contemplating look on his face.

"So…" Mason says.

Gavis shakes himself. "Ah, yes. I suppose we should get on with this. Shall we?"

"Yes," Mason agrees.

"Well, the fact of the matter is, I'm taking Sara with me and you're staying here. If you try to stop me, I will kill you. If you try to follow us or find us, I will kill you." Gavis claps his hands together. "That's simple enough for you to understand, isn't it?"

"I'm not letting her go," Mason says.

"Well, that's a pity." Gavis shakes his head. "I really don't want to kill you, boy, but you're not giving me many options."

He starts towards Mason, walking in a lazy manner that seems more threatening than anything else he could have done. Mason backs around the table, away from him.

"Your wife would let us go," he says.

Gavis stops for a second, narrowing his eyes. "If you know what's good for you, you won't mention her again."

"Who, Abby? That's what she goes by now. She's a really nice woman. She told me all about you and her and your failed marriage." Mason smiles humorlessly.

Gavis materializes right in front of Mason and grabs his shoulder. Mason's body goes rigid, and Sara lurches against the handcuff. She's not sure what Gavis is doing to Mason, but it's enough for him to sink to his knees under Gavis' hand, as if he is trying to withstand a great weight.

Gavis steps back, rolling up his sleeves. Mason falls onto his hands; his breathing becomes ragged.

"That's only a taste," Gavis snarls. "Talk about her once more and it will be thousands times worse, I promise you."

Sara watches Mason struggle to say something as Gavis turns, coming toward her. She tries to catch his gaze, not understanding why he's doing this. He'd never done anything violent before, not that she's ever seen.

He refuses to meet her eyes, looking down at the floor instead. His hands—normally so caring and gentle—are balled into tight fists, the tendons standing out against his pale skin.

"Gavis, please," Sara begs.

"Yes, listen to her, Gavis," Mason calls. "Look what happened when you never listened to Abby when she needed you to."

Sara's eyes stay on Gavis. Dread chills her heart as she studies his still form. His signature hat is dipped low over his face, shielding his expression from her. Sara doesn't know what Mason's talking about, but Gavis seems to.

He turns, striding over to Mason. His stance would seem casual if not for the tension in his shoulders.

Mason, who's just gotten to his feet, takes a shaky step away from Gavis, in an obvious attempt to escape.

Gavis reaches out, ignoring the hands Mason uses to protect himself, and takes hold of him again. Mason grabs Gavis' arm, hitting the floor immediately.

Sara tries to struggle to her feet, but the cabinet is so low she has to stay bent at the waist. She tries desperately to free herself, or at least see what's going on, but all she can see is Gavis' back and all she can

238

hear is Mason's muffled scream. The cell phone skitters across the floor, unnoticed.

Gavis steps back. He wipes his hands on his suit coat, shaking his head.

"This is your last warning, boy," he says. "Get out now. Forget about her, forget about me. This isn't about you!"

Mason staggers to his feet. He clutches the back of a chair for support, his face pale, gleaming and terrible.

"What is it about?" he grinds out.

"Saving people! Think of what I could accomplish if I took away all emotions. Think of the technological advances that could result, all the hate wars and crime that would end, all the violence and pain. It would just stop!" Gavis shouts.

Sara jumps at the sound. She can't ever remember seeing him this agitated before. He seems almost desperate, as if he needs to force Mason to understand him.

"You're willing to surrender everyone's good emotions for that?" Mason asks.

Gavis spins away, facing Sara and putting his back to Mason. He takes a few steps closer to Sara, meeting her gaze for the first time since Mason broke in. Her eyes trace the lines etched in his face, lines of agony and distress. His wild green eyes dart over her expression. She wonders what he sees there, what he feels when he looks at her now.

"There are no such things as good emotions. All feeling turns sour at some point," Gavis says softly. "Love turns to hate and compassion vanishes. No one with emotions is safe."

Sara tugs at the handcuff half heartedly. "Gavis?"

She doesn't know what she is asking, but it seems important. His eyes clear the more he looks at her, his expression transitioning from passionate to mournful. His eyes gleam, and Sara realizes that he's about to cry.

"All I wanted was to keep you safe," he whispers. "Can't you see that?"

"You can't save them. They won't bring back your daughter," Mason replies.

Gavis' eyes close in defeat. Sara watches him reach up and gently remove his hat. He sets it on the counter beside him, turning so Sara can finally see Mason.

He's not looking at her, but rather at Gavis. His expression isn't what she expected; it's closed, resigned, calm, as if he already knows how this is going to turn out. His shoulders are pushed back, his chin lifted. He is more confident and sure than Sara has ever seen him.

Gavis materializes in front of Mason. He shakes his head, holding his hand out in a gesture of compromise. Mason hesitates before clasping Gavis' outstretched hand. Gavis' touch has no negative effect on Mason. Relief floods Sara's body, leaving her weak.

"You are a good man," Gavis tells him. "In any other circumstance, you'd be so good for her. I respect you."

"I love her," Mason says simply.

"I know," Gavis replies.

Something seems to go wrong. Mason's expression becomes confused. His breath explodes outward, as if he's been punched in the stomach. Pain flashes over his features but he keeps his eyes locked with Gavis'.

He sinks to the floor. Sara finally finds her voice and starts screaming, not wanting to acknowledge what she knows is true. And there's nothing she can do to stop what's already started.

Gavis yanks his hand away from Mason's, taking a step back. Sara can't see his expression, but she quiets down at the change in him. She whimpers, tears starting to streak down her cheeks.

"You're a…a…" Gavis swallows loudly. "Oh, my God. You're a black hole."

Mason, his face blank, lies quietly on the floor. He says nothing and shows no sign of even registering what Gavis has said.

"Gavis!" Sara screams. "Gavis, no! *No!*"

Sara's hair shifts off her shoulders as a wind picks up in the middle of the apartment. A purple dust coats everything, something Sara's never seen before in all her years of dealing with these people.

Gavis focuses on something behind Sara. "How can you still love me? After what I've done?"

"I forgive you," is her only reply.

Sara pulls one last time on the handcuff. The metal screws groan, the faux wood breaks and she's finally released.

She's propelled into Gavis' arms, but she fights him, a scream bursting from her throat. Gavis' tries to restrain her, ignoring her flailing arms.

"Sara! Sara, there's nothing you can do," he says.

"You're lying!" she shouts.

"Sara—"

"Gavis, let her go."

Gavis does as Abby asks, and Sara falls to her knees, pulling Mason to her. He seems lifeless, but she can hear faint breathing.

"I didn't want it to end up like this," Gavis says.

Sara can hear Abby quietly reply, "She knows." The kitchen falls silent. Without turning around, she knows that they're gone, jumped to some unknown place far, far away from this tragedy he created and has failed to fix.

Sara pulls Mason's head into her lap, smoothing his hair back. "Mason?"

His eyes make an effort to focus on her face. She leans down and kisses his forehead. His mouth moves, but she has to strain to hear what he's saying.

"911."

Sara remembers what he asked her to repeat to him before all this happened, and she looks around wildly. She catches sight of the phone under the table and dives for it, letting his head *thunk* against the floor.

She doesn't see it, but his head rolls to look at her and he grimaces. He watches her wail into the phone, probably deafening the operator on the other end. He already knows that there's no help for him. He understood that before he came here. It is all part of the plan.

"Love… you…" he whispers.

His eyes close softly, his body finally relaxing.

×××

The ambulance jerks, running over the curb before slamming back onto the pavement, screeching to a halt. Two men and a woman grab their bags, slamming doors and relaying information to each other. They've done this many times, this race between life and death, and

244

they trust each other. Their feet slam the pavement as they dart efficiently into the apartment building.

Not one of them notice they've stepped on a child-like chalk drawing, one of a little blonde-haired girl with a pretty pink dress and a dark-haired boy wearing Chuck's All-Stars.

Part Eight

Slowly, like an elderly man finishing a crossword puzzle with a pen, time seems to slip away. Months? Years? It doesn't matter. It's like floating. Or like dreaming without actually experiencing a dream. He knows everything and not enough. He has a sense of self, but cannot actually find himself. Everything is pale colors and thoughts on marijuana. It's almost like swimming in velvet.

Just as slowly, memories begin to surface. Faces, names, dates, and words drift in and out like a television with bad reception. Then comes hearing. That is always the first physical sense to come back. The sound of a piston. The steady beeping of a tired machine. Like a depressed version of a techno song, it rings through, loud and clear.

Then feeling. Pain, lurking in dark places as if subdued by a heavy fog. An old friend who he doesn't like and never trusts but can't seem to shake. Like the stalker of a movie star, Pain lies in wait for a chance to ensnare his victim again.

Instinct whispers from the corner of his mind: *You can't go. Open your eyes to the light. Find the surface and know what it is truly like to survive.*

But he can't, no matter how much he tries. Like his old self is hollowed out and a mini replica of him is running around inside, screaming for help, desperate for contact. Knowing where his lips are, but not finding them to speak.

Eyelids flutter open, cracking away days of sleep and pain.

Mason's head is cocked to the side. He licks his lips, which feel swollen, and squints to bring into focus the words printed on a small, plastic bag directly in his line of sight. The letters stop moving just enough for him to catch up.

Morphine.

He traces the tube from the bag down a metal pole, to the floor. It's out of sight for just a moment before he realizes it snakes onto the bed, ending under a bandage in the crease of his elbow.

He takes a deep breath. Then another. A tube is under his nose and he fingers it, wincing. But it doesn't make sense to him, any of it.

His first thought is, *I'm alive*. His second: *It wasn't part of the plan*.

The room is dim, only showing the muted dawn—or is it dusk?—filtering in through two large windows. Everything is quiet, and it gives him time to try and concentrate. His mind feels slippery, as if it's been dunked in a vat of baby oil. He can't quite grasp it.

His head swivels. As he looks around he takes another deep breath, even though it's beginning to cause a stinging pain in his chest.

And there she is.

She's folded herself up in a chair, knees tucked to her chest and hands clasped together under her cheek. Her hair is tossed across her face, cloaking it from his view. He's surprised to note she is wearing a pair of jeans and a red t-shirt.

He's still fuzzy around the edges, but he's able to feel the expanding of his heart for her. But, unsure of how to speak or even move very well, he lies there mutely and just observes.

He stays like that for a long time, while the sun begins to slip into the room with increasing strength. Mason still cannot feel the passing of time, though he acknowledges it. The only sounds are the piston— which he understands is pushing the oxygen through the tube and to his nose—and the machine that keeps track of the beats of his heart.

Eventually, as the sun begins to blind him, Sara begins to stir. She shifts, causing one of her feet to flop over the edge of the chair. This causes her to sit up, waking.

When she opens her eyes and focuses on his face, the breath seems to explode out of her. For another slow, long moment, they simply watch each other.

A word hitches itself to a breath and struggles out of his dry throat. "Hey."

Sara bursts into tears, practically falling off the chair as she snatches up his hand and presses it to her face. She scoots closer to the top of the bed, pressing her lips into his palm, fighting for calm.

252

"Don't cry," he tells her.

"You died," she sobs.

"I know."

"I thought I lost you." Her words send her into another category of hysteria.

She's squeezing his hand way too tight for any kind of comfort, but he doesn't say a word. They stay like that for a long time, Sara seeking refuge in his simple touch, eyes screwed closed. Mason simply watches her, his body too weak for him to do anything else.

That's all the time they're allowed, as nurses bustle in to take care of him. Sara never leaves, but is shooed back to her chair, where she waits anxiously, wringing her hands. She never takes her eyes off Mason, and wears an overprotective expression as she watches the hospital staff.

"Not so discreet, is she?" the older, plumper nurse whispers to Mason.

Mason offers her one glance before his gaze shoots back to Sara. "She's never been one for it, no."

The nurses quickly finish, leaving with the promise of being back soon after calling the doctor and Mason's

mother. The door clicks shut softly and Mason smiles at
Sara.

"Come here," he says softly.

Sara hesitates. "You're not... I could..."

"I'll be fine."

She doesn't argue further, as desperate for the
contact as Mason is. She tucks herself gently into his
side, noting his wince as she brushes his ribcage. After
a few minutes of rearranging, they work out a system
where Mason can rest comfortably.

"You're wearing my clothes, aren't you?" he asks.

Sara's cheeks color. "Your mother brought them for
you. But I was here so long and the nurses insisted I
take a shower."

He takes her hand, running his thumb over the back.
He stares at the place where her string used to be,
looking for any sign of its existence. He can't find any;
it might as well have been a dream.

"Your plan worked," Sara murmurs. "Whatever
plan you hatched with Abby worked."

He can sense the questions in her tone. "Abby came
to me after you'd been taken. Asked what I would do to

254

save you. Said it would take me dying to truly set you free."

"So you knew then?"

"Yes, I knew."

She's quiet for a few seconds. "You knew you'd be killed and you came anyway."

"Anything," he nuzzles her hair. "Anything for you."

"When you died, I thought I'd died as well," she replies flatly.

He draws back and ends up wincing. "Don't talk like that."

"It's the truth." Her eyes are slightly accusing. "How would you have felt, if I'd died to save you?"

"You wouldn't have. I wouldn't have let you," he says firmly.

"Like you could stop me anyway. You don't have any idea what it was like—"

As she falls silent and looks away, Mason's not quite sure what to say. How could he ever make this up to her?

He can only think of one thing. "I love you."

"I know," she sighs.

"Well, gee, don't sound so ecstatic about it."

She looks up at him and sees his troubled eyes. He shifts around her and winces, trying not to tug on the IV in his arm.

"If you wouldn't squirm so much it would hurt less." Her voice is clipped.

He rolls his eyes. "Thank you, Captain Obvious. With your kind words of wisdom, I can now rest easily."

"Your sarcasm isn't necessary, Mason."

"Yeah, well, I died and just woke up in a hospital to the girl I loved going from smitten to incredibly pissed off." He glares at the inoffensive wall. "It wears on a guy."

She puts her long fingers under his chin, pulling his face back to hers. "I am smitten. Pissed off, yes. But smitten nonetheless."

Maybe it's the drugs or perhaps her admitting she loves him that makes him feel as high as the sun; he doesn't know which. It doesn't really matter, though, not to him. Not now.

Eventually she looks away. He watches her twist the thin bedspread in her fingers before he kisses her forehead. They're quiet for a while, his nose against her temple, both listening to the sound of his heart beating on the out-of-date machine.

"I'd do it again, you know," he comments slowly.

She smiles slightly. "I know. I've thought about it a lot these past few days and I've decided it's one of the things that makes me attracted to you."

"*What?*"

"You've been in a coma for several days—"

Sara takes a breath to continue, but Mason shakes his head, interrupting her. "No, no, no. I'm talking about your... *attraction.*"

"Oh." This seems trivial to her.

He waits for her to go on. "Well?"

"Well, what?"

"I dunno. I just thought you were too... innocent. You know, for that kind of thing." He blushes as he registers what he's saying.

"Oh, I already know all about sexual intercourse and everything. I'm innocent, not naïve."

Mason goes from blushing to a beet red. His neck gets hot. "Well, then."

"Well, you don't think Gavis shielded me from all that did you? I did watch television, you know," Sara continues. "That doesn't matter anyway. What does matter is that a girl stopped by the day after we came here. She said she was a friend of yours."

Mason's brow creases. "What girl?"

"She never said her name, but she gave your mother a bouquet of these really pretty blue flowers." Sara shakes her head, pulling a paper out of the pocket of her jeans. "She also gave me this."

Mason takes it from her, looking at it. "An address?"

Sara nods solemnly, staring at the inoffensive paper. "She told me it's where my mother lives. She told me that she's still alive."

Mason runs his thumb over a little doodle of a flower in the corner of the page. Even though the writing is in purple ink, the flower is in blue. He reckons he knows who Sara's new friend is.

"Abby told me about your mom when she told me what to do to save you. How do you feel about it all?" he asks gently.

"I don't know. I've been away for a long time. Perhaps she won't want me. Maybe she's moved on. She was severely depressed back then; she could have committed suicide for all I know." Sara sighs, twisting her fingers with Mason's.

"I don't think Abby would have mentioned it if she thought your mother was dead. And Mo—the girl who brought this paper to you—can see the future. I met her before I went to Gavis' apartment. I think she knows what she's talking about." Mason stifles a yawn. "Have you seen Abby lately?"

Sara shakes her head. "Not since… well, you remember. The girl—um, Mo told me they had to lie low, because the police would be after Gavis for… Anyway, I haven't seen her. I don't think I will see her again, actually."

"Really? Why not?"

"I can't explain it. It's just a feeling, I guess."

He snorts. "I just can't believe Abby got back together with him. I mean, after what he did to you? To those other girls?"

"He thought he was doing some good!" Sara replies defensively. "You can't blame him for doing what he thought was right."

"I can, and I will. Please don't tell me you're sticking up for him." He shakes his head.

"Look at it this way; without Gavis doing what he did, I never would have found you. Puts things in a different perspective, doesn't it?" She smiles.

"Yeah, I guess," Mason replies grudgingly. "Anyway, you said my ma gave you my clothes. I was wondering about her... about the kids."

Sara twists their fingers together. "They're fine. Apparently Abby dumped her bank account into yours, so you'll be good for a while. Everyone's fine; just worried about you."

"How long is awhile?" he asks.

"It's a pretty large number," Sara shrugs.

Mason's eyebrows shoot up. "No joke?"

"No joke," Sara promises.

They talk lightly about what's been going on with his family, and how he feels with his injuries. Eventually, as the nurses stop coming and the sun stops slanting so violently in the window, they lapse into a comfortable silence, just enjoying each other's company.

Sara continues to play with his fingers long after they've stopped talking. She thinks of her mother. She's not sure how she feels about it now, but she firmly believes that she and Mason could build a family together.

Mason, on the other hand, is making plans. If his family has enough money to support themselves without his help, he could continue to work and get his own apartment. He wonders where Sara would like to live and if he could continue working at Sven's if they decide to get a place closer to her mother's. He knows the neighborhood from the address Sara showed him, and it's a fairly good distance from Sven's, even with his biking abilities. He then wonders if he can get a car. He grins.

"What are you thinking about?" Sara asks quietly.

"The future," he responds. "Do you think it will be good?"

"With you? Fantastic." She smiles.

Mason kisses her forehead. "I was thinking the same thing."

Part Nine

The sun shines brilliantly through the trees on the side closest to the road, with beautiful, old buildings standing proudly behind, only a sidewalk separating them. Fall has begun to leave its mark, filling even the highest branches with flame-colored leaves.

The old sidewalk—covered with leaves the trees have already discarded—is being quietly abused along this small-town road. Children are hoisting heavy backpacks on their way home, business women on cell phones clack their way to the bus stop in heels, a few joggers stop at the intersection, bouncing in place and counting the beats of their pulse.

Four new bicycle wheels make their way here, dodging the people who claim the walkway as their own. They turn right at the end, keeping close to the row of buildings and picking up speed as they head down the hill.

After a few more minutes of town, the bikes make their way through a generous amount of countryside. The riders' breath begins to labor, even though the pair has been riding together for several months now. They never slow their pace, making good time.

They swing wide and enter a small housing development to the right. They slow, passing shiny new cars in driveways, lawns that still hold their healthy greenness, even with the onset of frost. Men in fleece jackets, fur gloves and hats hold open black trash bags as their teenage sons rake up leaves and drop them down into the plastic net. Teenage girls huddle together on porches and watch boys in the opposite yards with appraising eyes. Smaller children in overstuffed jackets waddle around in small groups under the monitoring gaze of their mothers.

It's a classic suburbia, so to speak.

The bicycles make their way to the end of the street, to a house that's obviously been painted within the last five years. The yard is overrun with leaves but is otherwise well looked after. The driveway is smoothly paved, the tar and cement mixture fresher than that of the road it connects to. A used car is parked there, slightly dented but with a survivalist attitude.

Bike stands are kicked down. Mason walks over to stand by Sara, who's pulling off her gloves and breathing on her fingers to warm them.

"You ready?" he asks.

She nods in reply, obviously nervous.

He murmurs something to her and pulls her in for a gentle kiss before opening a backpack and removing a little doll. Sara takes it from him, looking over the yellow yarn hair and one button eye. She suddenly feels calmer, ready for whatever this visit might hold.

Her pink Converse All Star's make their way to the porch, creaking up the two rickety stairs easily and making their way to the front door. Mason's staple red Chucks follow right behind. This is a place where his feet have never been, but hers remember it as if it was just yesterday.

Sara knocks on the door three times.

They stand for several minutes, Mason just behind her, their breath making clouds of condensation in the air before disappearing. He takes her hand and squeezes it. The only sounds are the voices of neighbors further down the street.

Suddenly, from the belly of the house, voices are heard. It's the laughing tilt of a woman and the deep reply of a man. The woman responds, laughing as she gets closer to the young couple on the porch.

The door jerks open to a woman, sporting a blonde ponytail, jeans and an FFA t-shirt, a smile on her face. She's instantly puzzled. "Can I help you?"

The speech Sara prepared for this moment dies in her throat. She can't think of a single thing to say. So, she holds out the doll.

The woman's expression changes completely, and she takes the toy slowly as if it might be an apparition. The woman touches the place where the doll's eye should be before looking up. When she finally speaks, her voice is only a cracked whisper. "Sara?"

"Hello, Mom." Sara smiles through watery eyes. "I have so much to tell you."

Acknowledgments.

*There are many, many people I have to thank for the first
publication of my first novel.*

*First and foremost, I have to credit God, for giving me the
talent, drive and ideas to work towards something so monumental.
Don't know where I'd be without Him, and that's the honest truth.*

*Secondly, a huge THANK YOU to Mrs. Homan, my sixth
grade teacher for forcing me to rewrite everything in Writing
Workshop and being the first to show me just how much I could love
words.*

*Also to Ms. Farrant who guided me through all my middle
school and high school years and for reading every poem, short story
and half completed manuscript I tossed her way. Without her advice,
both as an editor and a friend, I wouldn't be half the writer I am today.*

*To my friends, who threatened my physical health everytime
I thought about giving up.*

To my parents, who I drive crazy 96% of the time.

*To the rest of my family, for all those interesting stories to
tell.*

*To Meghan Tonjes, Alex Day, Tom Milsom, Alan Lastufka
and Charlie McDonnel for providing me with music to inspire me and
get me through those writer's blocks.*

*To Kaleb Nation for all his late-night BlogTv's and Q&A
sessions. For being a teen author, a role model and a hero to so many.*

To anyone who ever dared to dream of Other Things.

*And, finally, to myself for having to put up with all these
people and their endless love. I wish I could go back three years and tell
myself: You did it, man. You really did it.*

Moriah Jane Howell is a golfer, a YouTube vlogger, a hobby photographer and, above all else, a writer. She writes not because she wants to be the Next Big Thing, but because it helps her to understand herself and the world around her with a finer clarity. Moriah currently lives in Central Pennsylvania with her mom, dad and spastic puppy, Nittany. She can be reached as *FlamingTaco1479* on YouTube, or as *onceuponataco* on Flickr.

SARA SIX STRINGS is her first novel.